Books by Crissy Smith

Were Chronicles

Pack Alpha
Pack Enforcer
Pack Territory
Pack Rogue
Pack Community

Shifter Chronicles

Birds of Prey
Bear Claw
Eye of the Tiger
Coyote's Kiss
Wolf Pack
Lion's Claim

Bloodlines

Bite
Control

Anthologies

What's Her Secret?

Single Titles

Designated Alpha

Pack Community

ISBN # 978-1-78686-185-6

©Copyright Crissy Smith 2017

Cover Art by Posh Gosh ©Copyright 2017

Interior text design by Claire Siemaszkiewicz

Totally Bound Publishing

Published in 2017 by Totally Bound Publishing, Think Tank, Ruston Way, Lincoln, LN6 7FL, United Kingdom.

Were Chronicles

PACK COMMUNITY

CRISSY SMITH

Dedication

This book is dedicated to my husband — the love of my life and my biggest supporter. It was a difficult year, but I love how much of a fighter you are. You make me proud to be your wife and I know you'll only grow stronger every day until you are fully healed.

Chapter One

Early evening heat surrounded Gray Mason as he stepped out of his Ford truck after pulling over to the side of the road. The sign in front of him welcomed him to Coyote Bluff, Texas, located in the panhandle of the large state, a place he had never visited before. But recent signs had narrowed down the location of Prince of felines to a couple of possibilities—one of them being the canyons surrounding the town.

After he'd spoken to the Alpha Council and the Pack Alpha for the west Texas area, arrangements had been made for Gray to investigate in Coyote Bluff. He'd been hearing rumors about the town that accepted any and all shifters since he'd begun to investigate the kidnapping. It would make since for whoever had taken the Prince to hide out in an area that was so remote.

Excitement rippled through his body at the thought of the search finally going somewhere after three very long months. While the idea of an entire town full of shifters unsettled him a bit, he would do everything in his power to finally end his journey and make his way home.

He surveyed the area directly around him, seeking anyone who might be a threat. Sensing no one near, he took out his cell phone and called his Alpha.

"Hey, Gray, I was starting to wonder if I'd hear from you today," Tyler greeted him.

Gray had to smile. Tyler would worry whether Gray called in or not, but Gray liked knowing that someone would at least notice if he went missing.

"Yeah, sorry about that, boss," Gray answered and leaned

against his tailgate. "Crappy reception down here."

"Just be careful. I contacted the sheriff there to let him know you would be stopping by in a day or so. He seems like an okay guy, but remember we don't have any ties there," Tyler warned.

"So he's not family?" Gray enquired, asking his Alpha in this way if the man was a wolf shifter.

"I don't think so. The town is supposed to be full of other shifters, but I just can't tell over the phone."

Gray grunted. It wasn't that he didn't like the others — he just hadn't met many. Most of his dealings were with the felines and those experiences had not been good.

"I'll check into the hotel tonight, get a run in and see what I can nose out before I meet with him tomorrow," Gray informed the other man.

"Just be careful. There is no wolf Pack there, but that doesn't mean that there are no wolves. You don't want to trespass against them before you know who you are dealing with. Especially without back-up."

"No problem. I'll stay away from any marked spots."

"Then call me tomorrow and get some rest," Tyler ordered.

"Will do." Gray hung up, still grinning. He had been away from his Pack for so long he was started to feel the loneliness more and more each day. While some wolf shifters had no problem going rogue, the true, deep comfort he found with his Pack mates had started to fade and it made him edgy. And an agitated wolf was never a good thing. He needed his family. He needed to get home soon.

Normally, he only shifted a few nights a month to let his animal out. The longer he was away from family, the more agitated both he and the wolf became. Running late at night seemed to be the only way he could calm himself, and even that didn't work like it had.

"Coyote Bluff," he mumbled under his breath as he climbed back into his truck. "Out of all the animals who in the world would pick a coyote to name a town after?" Gray didn't know any coyote shifters, although he was aware they existed. Rumor had it that coyote shifters were more than a little crazy. If he had time maybe he'd be able to dig into the history of the place. Gray loved learning about different communities and their unique quirks.

He pulled back onto the main road and followed directions on signs until he found what he'd been looking for. The hotel had the appearance of an old cabin from the pioneer days. He parked in front of the door and got out, pleasantly surprised to see that while it might seem old, it was a sturdy building. The railings spreading from the entrance to both sides were composed of thick pieces of wood with delicate carvings.

A closer look revealed that the carvings were of several different animals. The detail — each species practically came to life — was simply amazing. There seemed to be more to this town than he'd first thought. That boded well for his purpose here.

He hefted his bag over his shoulder and pushed open the large oak door. The spacious entrance seemed to invite him in and Gray found himself smiling.

What greeted him first was the scent of fresh cooking. He'd been living out of convenience stores and on fast food for so long that his mouth watered as he thought about a hot, home-cooked meal. His stomach rumbled in agreement.

"I guess that means the first order of business will be getting you something to eat," a tall, slender woman said, coming to his side, laughing.

Gray grinned at the pretty middle-aged woman. "Didn't realize I was so hungry until I smelt whatever that delicious food is."

The woman laughed again, throwing her head back. "Oh no, Claude does all the cooking around here. But I will tell him you said that. I'm guessing you're Mr. Mason?" she asked and guided him to the small, neat reception desk he hadn't noticed. "I'm Dorothy. Claude and I own this place, so if you need anything, you just give me a holler."

"Yes, ma'am. Gray Mason here to check in and hopefully check out dinner."

"Oh, I am going to like you, Mr. Gray Mason," she told him, patting his hand. "Just sign this registration form. We will charge your credit card when you check out. The dining room is open from five in the morning to eight at night. But if you want anything when it's not open, you just let me know and I'll show you around the kitchen. It's open to all our guests. We get a lot of business in the dining room from the town folk, so don't you worry about what time you eat. We've got plenty to feed everyone."

Gray nodded and signed the paper she'd given him. The heavy welcome card he slid back across the counter to Dorothy reminded him of the old paper his grandparents had enjoyed. The pleasant memory brought him a touch of his past. What an unexpected gem he'd found in this odd town. "If all your food smells like this, I don't see myself eating anywhere else," he said. He had a feeling the meals there would also remind him of a time he'd never get back.

"There are places to grab food in town, also. We have a café, a coffee shop, a bakery, the pizza joint and even a steak house on the other side of town heading out. All good food, although no one cooks like my Claude."

"Now, Dorothy, I think you may be a little biased." Gray turned as a heavyset man joined them. He smiled and seemed friendly, but it was the power behind his eyes that told Gray much about him.

This was a shifter. Not wolf or feline, but something just as powerful. Gray stiffened and faced the man directly. He had hoped to avoid any display of dominance.

The smile fell from the other man's lips as he held out his hand. "Claude Gentry."

"Gray Mason, and Dorothy is correct. It smells amazing," Gray told Claude as they shook. While his wolf might have been straining to get out, Gray was professional enough to control his instincts. Being a detective in a very human world had tested him enough.

As soon as the words left his lips, he felt the change in the other man. Instead of a mood to match the cautious handshake, the man returned to his joyful self. "Well, thank you, son. Let Dorothy get you checked in so we can feed you," he told Gray with a friendly slap on his back.

Gray looked back to the woman in time to see her send Claude a worried glance before smiling at him once more. Gray breathed in deeply, trying to place any familiar scents. The woman was human, although she smelled like Claude. But he just couldn't place the other man. The scent was more fresh air and fields than the wild and woodsy scent of wolves.

He couldn't come right out and ask without sounding rude, so he just pushed it to the back of his mind as he accepted his room key and listened to the directions to his room.

Passing through the cabin—he no longer thought of it as a hotel—he appreciated the beauty and comfort of the décor and feel. He liked the little place already.

His room was located on the second floor, which suited him fine. He wasn't usually picky but being in a strange place surrounded by so many different scents had him on edge. Being on the third or fourth floor would have put him farther away from escape.

Later, maybe after my run, I'll calculate how many exits will get me to safety if need be.

When he reached his room, Gray took a minute to breath in the scents around his door. He didn't catch that any other shifters had passed by recently. Dorothy's pleasant aroma was all he found. Relaxing a little more, Gray put the key in the lock before pushing open his door. It amused him that the cabin didn't use the key cards most hotels had switched over to.

Stepping inside the space that would be his home for the near future, he nodded in approval. Clean and comfortable. There might not have been a lot of furniture—just a large bed, a couple of night stands, desk with chair and a long dresser—but it would suit his needs.

Instead of unpacking, Gray wanted to get back down to the dining room. He'd really grown hungry and it had been a long drive.

He dropped his bag onto the bottom of the bed then spun around to stroll right back out of the door.

Gray reached the bottom of the stairs and found Dorothy standing there, apparently waiting for him.

"I didn't think it would take you long to head back down here, so I had Claude start making you a plate," she said.

"I appreciate it, ma'am."

"Now." She waved her hand. "None of that. We're family here. You just call me Dorothy."

"Only if you call me Gray."

"It will be my pleasure," she said. Dorothy threaded her arm through his, urging him to the entrance of the dining hall.

There were already several couples eating who checked him out when Dorothy escorted him in. A few glanced up but only smiled before returning to their meals. Gray was taken back by the easy acceptance from other shifters.

He'd really underestimated Coyote Bluff.

"Now, you sit here by the window. As the sun sets, you'll have a great view of our wonderful town," Dorothy told him when they'd reached the spot she wanted him to take.

"Sounds perfect." Gray pulled out the chair and sat before Dorothy could do it for him.

"Now what do you prefer to drink?"

"An ice tea would be perfect."

"Sweet or unsweet?"

Gray laughed. "In Texas? I'm going to go with the sweet tea."

Beaming, she patted his shoulder. "Good man."

She was off in a flash, surprising him. Dorothy moved quickly, almost as if she floated.

Movement in the corner of his eye caught his attention and he leaned forward, trying to see what it was. A small animal darted between two cars, but he couldn't tell what it had been.

"Here you go, Gray." Dorothy set down his glass then a plate full of barbecue ribs, potato salad, green beans with bacon and cornbread.

"Oh, my God!" He bent forward, breathing deeply. He hadn't even ordered, but Dorothy had brought him exactly what he'd been craving.

"Enjoy!" Dorothy told him before leaving him to his overflowing plate.

Gray dug in, concentrating on filling his stomach with the best food he'd ever tasted. If anyone was watching, they'd probably think he hadn't eaten in months and Gray wouldn't have blamed them. He barely took the time to swallow. It was so fucking good.

Dorothy stopped by once to refill his tea while looking pleased with his progress.

It wasn't until he lifted his head that he noticed most of the other patrons had finished and left. The sun wasn't completely down, but it was most definitely dusk.

"You ate every bit," Dorothy commented with pride. "That will make Claude very happy."

"You must tell him that I enjoyed every bite. Best food I've eaten in years."

"I'll do that." She set down a bottle of domestic beer. "Now why don't you take this and sit out on the porch. Take in the sights and relax."

Gray stood and kissed her cheek, letting impulse take him over. He wasn't naturally a touchy-feely kind of guy, but the moment seemed to call for it.

"You'll fit in her perfectly." She patted his face and, if he wasn't mistaken, her eyes were damp. "Just perfectly."

Gray nodded, feeling embarrassed by his actions, before picking up his beer. He high-tailed it out of the dining room toward the side entrance where he'd spotted some nice-looking wooden seating.

Despite the name, Coyote Bluff was a gorgeous town.

He always felt better being surrounded by the woods and forests of home, but the canyons that surrounded him now had their own charm. He couldn't wait until later when he would be able to change forms and run.

But for now, as he waited for the evening to pass, he dropped down into one of the many chairs on the porch and kicked back. The restlessness that he had felt since before he'd arrived calmed and peace settled deep inside him until his eyes started to droop and he let himself drift.

It was the light sound of footsteps that kicked his instincts into gear and had him popping his lids back open. Just off to the side at the porch steps stood a little boy, about five or six, staring at him.

Gray dropped his feet onto the deck and nodded in the kid's direction.

Taking that as an invitation, the little boy scrambled up the steps to hover over him. "I'm Julian, I live next door, my aunt said I could come over and get some cookies from Claude, he makes really good cookies and he always saves me some."

The words flew so fast and with such a heavy southern accent that Gray actually had to think about what had been said. Once he put it all together, he grinned. His Alpha had a young daughter, so he'd had some dealings with small children. "I haven't had the cookies yet, but I hope you'll save me one."

The boy started to nod immediately. "I will. I promise."

Before Gray could respond, the boy scrunched up his face and sniffed. He knew the child was scenting him and, while it would have been rude from an adult, he had a feeling the young boy he had just met didn't worry about things like that. Discreetly, he breathed in the boy's scent as well.

He was shocked to smell cat.

"You smell funny!" Julian told him, leaning closer.

Gray couldn't hold in a laugh at the boy's exclamation and puzzled face. Once he quieted down, he knew that no matter what species Julian was, the kid was all right.

"I don't think I smell that bad. I took a shower earlier," he teased.

This caused Julian to shake his head so quickly he almost fell over. "No, you don't smell bad—just funny."

So he hadn't smelled another wolf before. That was interesting.

"Well, I'm a wolf, so maybe that's it," Gray offered.

And found himself with a lap full of kid.

"You're a wolf!" Julian squealed. "A wolf! That is so cool! I always wanted to meet a wolf. Daddy says that when I'm bigger I'll be able to meet everyone, but right now it's not safe."

Gray took in the boy's pout and pleading eyes and patted his back reassuringly. "You should listen to your dad—he seems like a smart guy. And right now it may not be safe, but hopefully when you're bigger it will be."

"But you're a good wolf, right? You won't eat me or anything?"

Gray forced back another chuckle. "No, I promise I won't eat you."

The child relaxed in his lap. "That's cool then. What's your name? Did you tell me already? I don't remember you telling me, but sometimes I don't listen too well."

"I think I might have forgotten to tell you. My name is Gray."

"Gray?" Julian chewed on his lip. "I like that. Is it because in your other form you're gray?"

It was a good question and kind of made Gray proud of the boy, which surprised him because the child was still a complete stranger. A feline. Oh well, he could puzzle over that later. Right now he was enjoying his new friend.

"Actually, I'm not gray at all as a wolf."

"Huh?" Julian thought about that.

"Well, little man? What are you?" Gray finally asked.

"Oh!" Julian jumped down so fast he almost toppled them both. But then he balled his hands on his hips and stuck his chest out. "I'm a bobcat!"

"Really?" Gray wouldn't have guessed that. Maybe that was why Julian's scent was a little different from the other felines he'd encountered. He had never met a bobcat before. Lions and one tiger, but Julian was his first bobcat, so Gray told him that.

"Really!" The kid squealed again. "That's so totally awesome!"

"Julian Jameson Williams!"

The boy and Gray both started as a woman rushed up the steps.

"I am so sorry, mister. I didn't know he was out here pestering you. He was supposed to run into the kitchen and be right back," she hurriedly told him, pulling Julian to her side.

Gray stood almost knocked back by the woman's beauty. She was probably in her early thirties, with bright green eyes and reddish blonde hair. She was quite a bit shorter than him and with her curvy body and ample breasts, he was embarrassed to find himself getting hard.

She stood in front of him in nothing fancier than old jeans and a tank top and he wanted to pounce on her. He took a step back just to be safe. It had been so long since he'd been that attracted to anyone.

"It's fine, really. I enjoyed visiting with Julian," he told her.

She smiled then, relaxing just a touch, and it took his breath away. The fact that the female had the scent of a cat didn't seem to bother his body or his wolf, who scratched to get out and play.

"Aunt Beth! Gray is a good wolf! He promised not to eat me," Julian told his aunt with all the innocence that could only come from one so small.

"Oh my! He didn't!" she exclaimed, hand going to her mouth.

Gray chuckled to show her he wasn't offended. "Yes, I did promise that and I always keep my promises, buddy."

Julian grinned back and finally the woman laughed.

"You'll have to excuse us. We haven't dealt with...with your...kind much," she stumbled, trying to explain.

Gray waved her off. "I understand. This is new for me, too. Julian is my first bobcat."

"Aunt Beth is a bobcat, too!" Julian added helpfully.

Gray had figured that but was glad to have it confirmed to him. That way he could get his head around the fact that, while she might be the sweetest-looking thing, she was still a cat and therefore still suspect.

"I thought I heard voices out here," Claude said, joining them on the porch. He carried a small plastic bag with him. "Beth called over to send Julian back, but I hadn't seen him. I take it you both have met our new guest?"

"Yes, Claude! And he's a wolf. But a nice wolf. He won't eat me."

Claude glanced over at Gray, who just nodded. Okay, it had been funny at first, but now he was starting to worry about all the wolf talk. He hoped it wasn't the same around town or he would never be able to get anything useful from the residents.

And he needed to find something there. They needed a lead.

Claude handed over the bag and Julian immediately dug in.

"Just one for now," Beth admonished.

Julian took one out then peered up at his aunt. "One for each hand?"

Beth shook her head before laughing. "No."

"Okay." Julian turned to him and held out the plastic sack. "One for me and one for my new friend."

Gray was touched. "That's very kind of you. Thank you, Julian." He selected the smallest treat so that Julian would get his fill later.

"You're welcome!" Julian exclaimed.

"We'd better get going." Beth tugged on Julian's arm.

"Bye, Mr. Wolf!"

"Good night, Julian." He dipped his head. "Ma'am."

"Night," Beth said quietly before her and Julian walked back down the stairs.

Gray watched for only a few seconds, aware that Claude was still by his side.

"He's a cute kid," Gray said.

Claude chuckled. "Julian's a handful and it takes all of us to keep that boy out of trouble, but he is also a gentle soul. I'm sorry if he disturbed you."

"He didn't," Gray assured the older man. "I enjoyed our visit."

"Good." Claude straightened his shoulders. "You were also very kind to Dorothy. I appreciate it."

Why do these people keep thanking me for being a decent person? What kind of wolf shifter have they met before? "Dorothy made me feel welcome and the meal was fantastic. I've been away from home a long time and this is the first time I've smiled and laughed in months. Everyone has been welcoming. I'm the appreciative one."

Claude gave him a firm nod before he slipped back inside.

Okay, things might not be as perfect in Coyote Bluff as he'd started to think. Which was a bit of a comfort since he was almost ready to claim them all to be some sort of pod people.

Gray retook his seat and kicked his feet back up onto the rail. He could barely see the porch of the house next door. Somewhere inside, Julian was probably eating his cookies with Beth. Gray wished he could've joined him. And didn't that bear some serious thinking?

Beth led Julian up the stairs to the second floor and his room, still thinking about the wolf shifter. It'd scared her to death when she had spotted her nephew right in front of the man. Every protective instinct she had in her had wanted to jump in front of the boy until the threat was gone.

Instead, she had been stunned at how open and friendly he had been. Not to mention handsome. Even as she'd crossed the yard, desire had battled her fear. But she couldn't afford to think like that. While her community might be built on tolerance of human and inter-species relationships, she was still a cat and he a wolf. Sometimes it wasn't meant to be, and, attracted or not, this was one of those times.

Well, maybe she could still think about those gorgeous eyes that had practically set her on fire. His built body and height hadn't hurt, either. *No one has to know, do they?* If he had been a cat, or any other species, she would have thought he'd make the perfect mate.

She sighed inwardly as Julian went on and on about the wolf next door. She would have to warn her brother that Julian was completely taken with the stranger. When Julian's naturally curious nature came out and he got this way, only time would divert his attention.

Together, the two of them followed Julian's nightly ritual of brushing teeth and getting ready for bed. Once her nephew was tucked in, she kissed his forehead. "Daddy will be home soon and in to check on you," she told him.

"Cool! I'll tell him all about my new friend!"

She smiled down at him, although she had every intention of beating him to it. That way, at least her brother would be a little more prepared than she had been.

Back downstairs, she made herself a glass of iced sweet tea and went to sit on the front porch swing. Her body still hummed happily after the encounter with the wolf shifter and, although she couldn't act on it, she thought she might as well enjoy it while she could.

Few wolves ever ventured into Coyote Bluff. Wolves tended to keep with their Packs and in their territory. The ones that had come by usually didn't last long. They were too dominating to leave things alone around the place, and while the people might be tolerant of one another, they were also protective. Their ways worked for them. And no one was going to let a rogue wolf come in and take over. A few had tried, but they were almost always quickly run out of town.

With the exception of one wolf, none had ever stayed.

Mark was a special case, though. The wolf was so tormented and afraid that he jumped at his own shadow. Even after a year of living in town, the wolf had hardly ever left his house and, as far as she knew, had never shifted. She wasn't completely sure what had happened to him and she never pressed. They had become friends, but she knew she was one of only a few. Julian had never met Mark.

The story about the feline Prince being taken had reached them when it happened. The town wasn't into the politics of the felines and others, but given the number of felines in town, they'd been asked to keep an eye out for anything suspicious. The rumor of the wolves helping search for him seemed to be true, if the reason for Gray's visit was really an attempt to assist with the rescue.

The sheriff, Joe, had told them that some of the searchers might be coming down, but Beth hadn't really thought any other shifter species would care about the Prince. Half of her *own* species didn't care. Cats were solitary creatures and while they did have a royal line that governed the big laws, most felines lived their own lives and didn't get involved in one another's business. It wasn't that way here in Coyote Bluff, though. The closeness of the community was what she appreciated about her home. She could live close to her family and wasn't expected to fend for herself. Very un-cat-like.

Her brother, Dawson, and Julian were the only close family members she had. Their parents had left them right after they had become adults. The oldest sibling — her and Dawson's brother, Casey — had joined the military and they hadn't seen him since. That had been twenty years ago. Luckily Dawson also felt the same way about having family close by, or she would be alone.

The headlights from her brother's patrol car bathed her in a spotlight as he parked. She scooted over on the swing as he stomped the dust off his boots then took a seat next to her.

"It's a nice night. I thought the heat would never break,"

he greeted.

It had been unusually hot for May. Already hitting the hundreds and summer wasn't even upon them yet.

She handed over her tea to share and nudged his shoulder. "Julian made a new friend."

Relaxing back into the wood swing, Dawson chuckled. "What is it this time? A fish in the pond or maybe a rat from the barn?"

Julian forever made friends with anything that moved. Shifter or regular animal, it didn't matter.

"Wolf shifter," she said quietly.

Dawson stiffened and paused, seeming to think about his words before he spoke.

"So he made it to town? Joe wasn't sure what day, but had thought within three."

She nodded. "Came in tonight. I didn't know he had arrived yet and Julian wanted some of Claude's cookies."

"And instead found a wolf?" Dawson guessed.

"Yep. When he didn't come right back, I went looking for him and found him on the porch of the inn."

Dawson inhaled—his way of getting himself to keep calm. She should probably stop teasing him, but what were sisters for?

"Damn it, Beth." His patience was finally up. "Do I need to kick a wolf's ass or not?"

Giggling, she slapped her brother's leg. "Nah, he promised not to eat Julian."

Dawson groaned. "Please tell me he didn't use those exact words."

"Oh, he sure did."

"Damn it," he groused. "I never would have said that if I'd known Julian would take it so literally."

She snorted, unable to hold back her amusement. "Well, Gray seemed pretty cool about it, if that helps."

Shaking his head, he stood. "If he's here for more than a few days, I can only imagine what else will be said. But I guess I'll find out tomorrow. Joe wants me to show Gray some of the trails. We don't think anyone has been past the barriers into the unused parts of the canyon, but really it's too big to know for sure. The park rangers are covering the public entrances."

"Is that why he's here? He thinks someone might be hiding in the canyon?" Usually her brother kept work to himself, but if he was willing to talk, she wanted to know. She had the same curious nature as her nephew.

"It's nothing to worry about," Dawson told her, switching back to 'big brother'. "If anyone is here, we'll find them for sure. It's been a long hot day. I'm going to work out before I shower."

"Okay. Now that it's cooled down, I might go for a run."

"Just be careful. Especially with a strange wolf in town."

"I promise not to be eaten by the big bad wolf, either," she teased.

Dawson rolled his eyes but went into the house without saying anything further. It was a good thing, because once she caught her own words, she blushed, thinking about one way she wouldn't mind being eaten by the wolf.

She sighed and set her tea down on the table. A run was a good idea. She could burn off some energy and hopefully not be up all night thinking about the sexy man next door.

Trails to the canyon area were all over town. It gave the residents easy access to let their animal sides loose. The public access to the canyon was on the other side of the area, with hundreds of acres in between. Even if they were spotted as animals, no one would be the wiser. And she could smell the humans before they would ever see her. Plus, the park rangers kept all bridges and roads to their area closed off. It helped that most of the rangers were shifters or related to one somehow.

That was how the community worked. They watched out for one another. Humans had the police. The shifters only had each other.

It was a short ten-minute walk to the clearing where she could shift. She climbed up and into the cave she and Dawson used, quickly shedding her clothes before becoming a bobcat.

She stretched, enjoying the pull on her muscles. Even though it had been less than a week since she'd shifted, it felt as though it had been much longer. She rubbed against the walls of the cave, giving in to the instinct to mark her territory. There were no other bobcats in the community other than her brother—and when he finally shifted, her nephew—but it still felt good to her cat to follow tradition.

Since she didn't actually like to run, but was more of a climber, she decided to head up to the top of the canyon so she could lie around under the moon. There was a small creek close by, too.

She started up, leaping and jumping as much as she could. Her curious nephew always asked how she felt when she got to shift, and as hard as she tried, she could never find the right words. It felt freeing, as if she was finally completely herself.

The thick foliage covered her as she stalked around, wishing for a playmate to pounce on. Sometimes her brother would come with her, but most of the time she was alone. Even other cats in town preferred to be by themselves. Her cat seemed to be missing that part of its personality.

A low tree branch offered her more fun as she climbed and chewed on it. As she started to scratch, she heard the yowl of a lone wolf not too far from where she was playing.

Planning on just getting a look at the wolf, she leaped from the branch and prowled toward the sound. It was less than five minutes before she caught a woodsy scent ahead of her. Crouching, she started crawling forward.

There, at the creek she had planned on visiting, stood a fully grown wolf. Her senses told her it was also a shifter, but she would have guessed that even without them since she knew how rare that type of wolf was. The red wolves were an endangered species, reported to total less than one hundred in America.

Looking at the animal, she was awed.

She squatted low to the ground to keep her hiding place as he dipped his head to drink from the clear water. *What a beautiful creature*, she mused as he stretched his neck back and howled again. Even though she was a cat, she still felt the loneliness that call conveyed. An answering rumble gathered in her throat and she had to hold herself back.

In the wild they were natural enemies. Even while human, she had never met a wolf who hadn't thought he was better than her.

With a heavy sigh, she laid her head down on the ground. She must have been louder than she'd thought, because his head snapped in her direction. She remained downwind so she knew he hadn't picked up her scent.

She tried to make herself as small as possible, belatedly realizing that spying on a wolf she didn't know wasn't the brightest idea she'd ever had.

To his credit, he didn't charge her. Instead, he tilted his head to the side and lowered himself much the same way she had.

She watched as he slowly crawled closer to her. When their gazes met, he stopped.

The same pull she had felt earlier returned and her muscles bunched as she waited.

He started toward her again, just as slowly and carefully, and she also scooted closer. They had started several yards away, but all too soon—and yet not soon enough—they were in the open with just a few feet separating them.

The wolf rolled to his side and pawed the ground. If she could have, she would have laughed. Instead the sound that came out of her was more of a small purr.

The wolf's ears perked up before he did it again.

So, as he'd asked, she moved to rest next to him. They didn't touch—just breathed in each other and shared the night. Side by side they stayed as the stars over them twinkled and the canyon sounds sang for them.

It was nice—peaceful, even—and she relaxed enough to close her eyes.

A whisper of a hot breath passed over her as the wolf bumped her chin with his head. She nuzzled into him without thinking.

The zing of awareness that shot through her body shocked her. He must have felt something too, because he jerked before nudging her again.

If they were in human form, she had no doubt they would be kissing. But as animals…

She jerked away. Damn it, she was a bobcat. There was no way she could have these feelings for a wolf. As carefully as she could, she inched away from him. He flopped back onto his stomach, watching her.

As he moved toward her, she swiped at him with her claws still sheathed. She didn't want to hurt him, but she had to get away.

What in the world had she been thinking? They hadn't just been playing — they were flirting, practically making out.

Once she had enough room to flee, she turned and took off. She didn't even glance behind her. Didn't dare. She just ran.

She scrambled down the canyon cliffs, not slowing until she got to her cave. Just as she reached her spot, she heard the heart-breaking sound of that howl.

Doesn't matter, she told herself. *We're from two different worlds.*

Chapter Two

Gray wasn't in the best mood when he woke the next morning. The interaction with the bobcat had kept him tossing and turning all night. He hadn't meant to scare her away. He hadn't meant for anything to happen at all.

But when he had heard a small rustle in the wind and had seen her, his brain had gone and he had been left operating on emotion. It had been so long since he'd been able to run with his Pack. The loneliness had gotten to him and he'd sent his call out to the wild. To find Beth in her other form there when he'd been so low had seemed like fate.

But he'd pressed too hard and too fast. She didn't even know him and yet he had wanted to cover her with his scent and have hers all over him — to make a claim.

He quickly ran though his routine, not even taking the time to relieve his morning wood. His hand had lost all appeal over the last few months, anyway.

He perked up a little at the wonderful smells from the kitchen once he got to the dining room.

"There you are!" Dorothy greeted him as he entered. She ushered him to the same table by the window. "I saved the best seat in the house for you. You have to see the world wake up from here."

It was a nice view of the canyon with the sunrise coming up. Dorothy made it even better by already accepting and welcoming him. The older human was a very special treat herself.

"I was worried you would miss the magical moment," Dorothy told him. She poured a cup of coffee from a tray and set it in front of him.

"Magical?" he enquired politely.

"You just watch. You'll see," she promised and patted his shoulder. "I'll go get your breakfast."

He opened his mouth to remind her that he hadn't ordered yet but she was already headed in the direction of the kitchen. Shrugging, he looked back out of the window. Maybe that was how they treated all their guests. Gray wasn't going to complain when the dinner he'd had previously was something he still couldn't believe he'd gotten to try. If he was in Coyote Bluff long, he'd have to up his fitness plan.

Unbelievable as it seemed, he was actually enjoying his visit. Maybe Dorothy knew what she was talking about with the whole table-seating thing. Gray found himself smiling as he peered out over the street to the scene beyond. That was when he saw it—the blending of colors as the sun hit the canyon surface. He leaned forward to try to catch every inch possible. Yellows, oranges, reds—all mixed together until the world before him came alive.

A bald eagle flew into sight and dipped low as if greeting the morning.

"It's pretty amazing, huh?" A deep voice interrupted his admiration.

Gray hated to pull his attention away but turned to greet his company. "It really is," he agreed.

The striking man in front of him wore a deputy's uniform. He was also a cat, and an older version of young Julian.

Gray stood and held out a hand. The man seemed shocked for a second but quickly schooled his face.

"Gray Mason," he introduced.

"Dawson Williams." They shook and Dawson motioned back to the window. "Not a lot of people get to witness Mother Nature coming alive. You should count yourself lucky."

Gray understood the underlined meaning of the words. He shouldn't wear out his welcome. "I do," he assured him.

"Sheriff Manor told us about your visit yesterday and

asked if I would be willing to show you some of the unmarked trails that might be worth investigating. Since I was here, I thought we could enjoy some of Claude's cooking while we discuss exactly what you're looking for," Dawson suggested.

"Well, then, please join me. Dorothy said she was bringing me some food…"

"She saw me come in. I eat here every morning, so she'll take care of me," Dawson explained. "But before we get down to business, I would like to get one thing out of the way."

Gray tried not to tense. After what had happened the night before with Beth, he had no doubt her brother would tell him to stay away. The man had every right to. They didn't know Gray. From what he'd gathered about the other wolves who'd visited, they had every right to wonder about his intentions. Hell, even *he* didn't know what his intentions were.

"I understand you met my son last night."

Gray nodded cautiously. "Julian."

Dawson surprised him by sighing. "He's a good kid. Curious and loves adventure, but I know he can be a little much. I would just appreciate it if he starts to bug you that you tell Dorothy, Claude or my sister Beth. They can keep him out of your hair."

"Honestly, I wasn't put out in any way last night. My Alpha has a daughter a few years older than him and, with my being gone so long from the Pack, Julian was actually a very welcome sight. You're right, though—he is a great kid."

Dawson seemed to relax. "Thanks, man."

Dorothy came back with two plates of food and a cup of coffee for Dawson. Once she'd refilled Gray's cup and was on her way to help someone else, Gray took in the food. Eggs, bacon, sausage, biscuits and gravy and hash browns covered every inch of the large plate. And the smell… He could have died and gone to heaven.

"Luckily they're used to serving shifters so every plate is always packed full to fill us up," Dawson told him with amusement.

"I've got to tell you, I don't eat this good at home," Gray shared.

The two men dug into their breakfasts. A comfortable silence settled over the table. Dorothy topped off the coffee as she walked by but never interrupted.

Once he'd stuffed his face and had mopped up the last of the gravy with a bit of biscuit, Gray patted his stomach and leaned back. "Damn, so good. I probably shouldn't have eaten all that if we're going hiking."

Dawson grinned over his own empty plate. "Now you know why I'm here every morning. We'll burn off the calories, though."

Gray smiled back and picked up his cup. He already liked Dawson. With Dawson's help, maybe he would finally be able to make some headway into the investigation. Dawson seemed like the kind of man Gray would enjoy working with, too. He got the feeling that Dawson was a straight shooter who protected his family and his community.

"So, Joe — the sheriff — said you had reason to believe that whoever took the Prince may have traveled through here, or might even still be here?"

"Yeah, there hasn't been enough evidence to really point out who they are, but we've come across a couple of their hideouts. We always seem to be missing them by a week or less, so some of the Alphas are worried we have a leak warning them before we get there."

Dawson nodded for him to continue.

"This last time, we tried to keep it as quiet as possible. But somehow they must have been tipped off, because they were gone when we got to the camp in Oklahoma. They'd only been gone a couple of hours and while they'd tried to burn all of their papers and stuff, they didn't get to it all before they took off. We were able to dig out some half-burned sheets and they were maps. One of the locations is the canyon."

"And the others?" Dawson asked.

"Some caves in New Mexico and a site down in the swamp near New Orleans. We split up and I came here. It might be nothing, but we have to check it out."

"Let me ask you this," Dawson said, lowering his voice. "Why do you care? What do the wolf Packs have to gain in finding him?"

It was a fair question and Gray would have been surprised not to have been asked. "That's tricky. Yes, the Prince had agreed to meet with our wolf representative to discuss him joining some of our Packs who will be going public. Just to meet—he hadn't said one way or the other if he would consider joining. That's tied into my motivation to help. By all accounts, the Prince was taken because he'd even agreed to meet. If we caused him to be taken because of that, it is our responsibility to help get him back."

"It wasn't your fault, though. Not the Packs' fault."

"Maybe not, but I still think that if we have to the resources to help find the Prince, then we need to step up," Gray said.

"And this is all because our Prince agreed to meet with one man?" Dawson pressed.

"I understand your doubt, but I've found that the question of going public or not hits a lot of people's hot buttons. Families, couples and friends are arguing about the issue. I think whoever took your Prince is trying to keep the felines out of the discussions."

Dawson shook his head. "I guess I'm just having a hard time understanding."

Gray paused and glanced back out of the window. "This is nice. The town, this community you all have here, protecting one another. It's like a Pack. But not everyone has that. We have several rogue wolves who don't have Packs, cats who are solitary and live alone, even other shifters who have no family at all. Little by little, they're being hunted down like their lives mean nothing. There's no one to protect those shifters. By becoming known to the world, we'll be able to bring awareness to those who would hunt us."

"You have strong feelings about this," Dawson noted.

"The natural wolves that share my breed are almost extinct. And while they are trying to reintroduce some into these parts, it'll never be the same. I also lost a good friend of mine about ten years ago. He was a gray wolf and was out hunting in protected lands. Two hunters killed him. They were busted and all they got was a slap on the wrist. They killed a *man*. Yes, he was a shifter, but he should have been safe there."

"I understand, but, without hunting, some animals will take over," Dawson argued.

"Yes, but if we have protected land to run in and the penalties are stiffer, then it's a start," Gray volleyed.

Dawson sat back and held up his hands. "I agree with you, man. And I think it's a good idea, but I wonder how it will work. What would keep people from kidnapping a shifter to try to become one themselves? We know that can't happen. You can't be bitten by a wolf or scratched by a cat and become a shifter. How do we prove that?"

Gray shook his head. "I don't know. Tony, the wolf who's the representative for the shifters and the government, says it's all about education. The government, or a select group of them, knows about us. Hell, some *are* us. He says that once we come out, everyone will be surprised by how high the support goes."

"Huh. Well, we aren't going to figure it out today. I brought an extra pack for you, so if you're about ready to head out, we can get started. Leaving this early, at least it isn't a hundred degrees."

Gray stood along with him. "I'm ready." He had dressed in jeans and a T-shirt, his old and worn-in hiking boots and had his ball cap stuffed into his back pocket.

The two headed for the door.

"I pulled my SUV in front this morning—" Dawson started.

"Daddy! Wolf!" Julian ran to the two men and threw

himself into his father's arms.

"Julian, his name is Gray, not Wolf," Dawson gently corrected the youngster.

"Sorry, Daddy. Hi, Gray!" Julian greeted, waving his arms frantically.

"Hey there, little man," he told the boy, patting his head, and Dawson put him down. He turned to the woman hovering in the background. "Good morning, ma'am."

Beth smiled and blushed a little, but thankfully seemed okay with him. "Good morning, Gray."

She was just as stunning as yesterday. Every feeling of rightness he'd had being in her presence returned. He stepped closer to her and was thrilled when she did the same. That was when he caught what the other two members of her family were talking about.

"Not today, son—Gray and I have to work. But we will be home for dinner. Why don't the four of us have dinner here tonight?"

"Really? Cool!" Julian was already excited.

Dawson glanced at Gray and he nodded. He wouldn't mind spending some time with the family. He really wanted to talk with Beth too.

"All right, then we better get going and you go have breakfast," Dawson told his son.

"Maybe after dinner you wouldn't mind taking a walk with me?" Gray asked Beth softly.

She darted a glance at her brother but nodded. "I think I would like that."

Elated, Gray grinned. He was taking a big chance, but he had to know if the attraction between them was a fluke or if Beth would even be interested in something with him. Not that he'd worked out exactly how that would happen. He was there to do a job, not find a date. Plus he wasn't actually going to be around long. That was going to be a worry for later, though. He and Dawson did need to get out to the canyons before it got too hot.

"See you later, Julian," he told the boy, walking past him.

"Bye, wolf Gray! See you tonight!" Julian hollered back happily.

Beth hushed him as she led him back the way they had come and the two men headed outside. The heat was already starting to rise as they reached the patrol vehicle.

Gray pulled on his cap, and his sunglasses from where they'd been hanging on his shirt, and climbed in.

"There's an old ranger station about a half mile down a back road. If these guys didn't want to come through town or the public entrance, that would be the best bet. It's overgrown but, if they were determined enough, they could get into the canyon that way."

As they drove, Gray got the first look at the town in daylight. Cute cobblestone streets covered the downtown area, with old-style black lamp posts on the corners and no traffic lights.

"Up ahead is the station. There we have the sheriff, Joe Manor, and two deputies—a human named Stan Davis, and me."

"Human?" Gray asked, surprised.

"Most of the town is either shifters or their families. All know about us so it's safe. Stan's brother is a mechanic. He's married to Tammie, who runs a hair salon named Foxy Ladies. She's a fox shifter."

"A fox?" Gray leaned closer to the side window as they passed first the station then, three buildings later, the salon. "I have to be honest—other than wolves and a few felines, I have never met any other shifters."

"I don't imagine you have. Most wolves stay within their territory and with their own kind."

Gray was about to defend his species, but Dawson cut him off. "And there is nothing wrong with that. Wolves stay together. It's one of the traits I admire most. The only family I have besides Julian is my sister. Everyone else has taken off to be on their own. Even Julian's mom left after a year."

"Oh man, I'm sorry to hear that," Gray replied honestly. If

he were lucky enough to have kids, he couldn't see himself ever leaving them.

"It's our way. I can't fault them, but I also don't agree. We are human also—I like to think more human than animal. So leaving your child, your family… I just don't…"

Gray let him trail off without pushing. The comfort he felt with the bobcat family was unusual. It also felt instinctual and he would just have to trust it. His Alpha had taught him to be aware of other shifters' thinking. Tyler was a big supporter of letting a shifter live the life they thought was best, but Gray had to agree with Dawson. Family was supposed to be forever. One shouldn't walk away from that bond for any reason. That felines lived solitary was one reason he didn't understand the species.

"Anyway, we moved here so Julian could grow up with other shifters and never have to worry about being picked on for being a small cat. The bigger species can be brutal about that."

There was a story there, but Gray let that pass as well.

"I don't know why I am telling you all this. I just really want you to understand how important this town is to me. This is a safe haven. Your comment about it being like a Pack was dead-on. If the people you are after are here, I want to help you catch them. Help you get the Prince back. But I don't want anything to hurt the town or its residents. My friends."

Gray glanced over at Dawson. Every emotion showed on his face. "I promise to do my best to protect the town and everyone in it. I've been on the road for three months now. This is the first time I wanted to stop and just rest without pushing twenty-four hours a day. There's simply something about this place, or maybe the people, that seems to calm me."

Dawson laughed, tossing his head back. "Careful, man— we might just keep you."

Gray smiled but was somewhat troubled. That was starting to worry him—the settled feelings that had been with him since he'd arrived. Back at home, things had changed. The Pack was growing. Some of the wolves in Colorado were moving around as his Alpha had decided to go public, while another Alpha — Austin, the mate of a good friend — had chosen to stay hidden.

Austin had made the best decision for his Pack and his family, and Tyler, Gray's Alpha, had made the best for his. But with Austin and Kiley mating and her moving away, Tyler's daughter Jesse growing up and himself getting older, Gray had started to feel life passing him by. He enjoyed working as a detective and with his Pack. But there was more to an existence than work. He just needed to finish his current mission before he could decide on the rest of his life.

"The ranger station is just up ahead," Dawson told him.

Gray found himself disappointed that they'd reached the spot so soon. He rather liked talking to Dawson and he still hadn't worked up the nerve to bring up anything about Beth.

The fact that Beth was still there with her brother and nephew was a good sign, but he didn't know anything about her except for the strong attraction between the two of them.

Dawson had commented that Beth had stuck around and was the only family he had besides Julian, but did that mean she'd never considered leaving?

He was putting too much pressure on himself about a woman he'd just met. Gray knew that but it didn't stop him from wondering and worrying. The entire trip had knocked him off-balance.

The old ranger station was indeed rundown, with overgrown foliage covering the building and drive. As Dawson parked, Gray peered out of the window, trying to see if anything had been disturbed.

"It's been about a week since the last rain," Dawson informed him as they exited the vehicle. "Tracks should be pretty easy to spot."

"We're only about three days behind them, so if they came through here, there might be some trail." Gray shared his hope.

"The building still seems secure," Dawson observed. "But let's check it out."

As they searched around the outside, Gray tried to breathe in and remember every scent for future use. Most of the smells were old, but a few — three separate ones — were stronger than the others and seemed to be newer.

"They didn't get inside, but I can smell strangers. Maybe up to five days old? Not sure, but I don't recognize them."

Gray nodded. Back behind the building was some broken and stomped-down vegetation. "You see that?" he asked, tilting his head.

Dawson followed his line of sight, backing away from the window he'd been trying to look through. "Let's go."

Slowly and soundlessly, they started the search. It wasn't a clear path — whoever had been through had been careful — but they were still able to get a mile from the station before they had to make a decision on which way to go. It helped that Dawson knew the area well.

"If it was me, I would head east to the caves. If they go too far west, they could run into tourists and the rangers. They might be able to blend in there, so it's still a possibility, but I just don't think they would risk it if they were trying to hide someone," Dawson offered his opinion.

"I trust your instincts. Let's head east, then," Gray agreed.

The trek up the canyon and closer to the caves was hard-going. They stopped after an hour and thirty minutes at the first of a series of caves to grab a drink and eat energy bars while they discussed a game plan.

"What do you think about shifting when we get closer? It would be easier to search. We can cover more ground and use our animal instincts to see if anyone has been through," Dawson suggested.

Gray took a swig from his water bottle. "That'll work for me."

"I, uh… I have shifted with others from town so I don't think my cat will have any issues, but will your wolf…?" Dawson asked, finishing with a wave from his hand.

Gray remembered the night before and smiled. "I think it'll be okay."

"Good." Dawson stood from where he had been sitting against a rock. "Let's get back to it then."

They gathered the wrappers and bottles and stuffed them into their packs. They climbed for another fifteen minutes before they came to a small group of trees with cover to hide their things.

"Let's start at the first cave and go from there. Once we get to where the paths intersect, we should get an idea if anyone has been through."

Gray nodded and he and Dawson started to strip. Gray ran often with his Pack so he had no problem getting naked in front of him. They separated a little when it came time to shift.

Only minutes later, he waited in his bigger wolf form for the bobcat.

Dawson jumped onto one of the large rocks and stretched. Gray shook his body, feeling the muscles move and pull. He loved his other form. He enjoyed the freedom of being able to shift into a wolf. It made him feel so powerful.

So many people in the world didn't get to share the same experience as him.

Dawson's earlier observation about humans wanting to experiment on a shifter to try to become like them was a valid concern. It was also the biggest reason shifters had remained hidden for so long. Times were changing, though, and he and his fellow shifters needed to adjust to the world around them.

Dawson vaulted down and joined him and the two of them took off at a slow run. They didn't want to use up energy they might need later. They'd had to leave the radio Dawson had carried with their clothes. No cell phone reception, so that wouldn't be able to help either.

The day was more for recon than anything else. If they came upon anyone, they would have to handle it with just the two of them. With enough time, if the Prince wasn't in immediate danger, or they had too big an area to cover, they could call in for backup.

They reached the first cave and Dawson went ahead. While he nosed around the opening, Gray watched his back, keeping every one of his senses open for any danger around them. Dawson glanced over at him and Gray nudged him to go on. He didn't smell any others around, so it should be pretty safe.

Gray stayed outside while Dawson searched the cave. After the bobcat came out and shook himself, they moved along to the next one.

It was another hour of searching, the two of them growing more and more frustrated, before they picked up a scent that should not have been there.

Gray smelled another wolf.

He lowered himself to the ground and growled low in the back of his throat. Dawson turned to him and followed his direction.

This was what they'd been searching for—a sign that someone had been up there. It could have just been a lone wolf, but Gray didn't want to take a chance.

Gray stood watch as Dawson moved farther up the canyon, which was becoming steeper until even Dawson had a little trouble with his footing. Gray stayed close, though, giving Dawson room but still offering the security he would need to concentrate on any scents.

The two of them followed the faint trail for another half an hour before Dawson stopped and rested. Gray sat close by, on watch. When he felt a nudge and Dawson dipped his head, he understood the message—to change back to human.

Once both men had gone from animal to human, they shared a troubled look.

"Wolf and feline," Gray shared.

"Yes, the farther up we go, it gets stronger." Dawson shook his head. "The beginning of the trail was a lot harder to find. Now that we're getting closer, it's like they're waving around their scents. I don't know whether they got careless or if they don't care if we find them."

"A trap, then?" Gray asked, as he'd had the same thought.

"I don't know," Dawson admitted. "But I have a bad feeling."

Gray nodded. "So do we turn around and get help or should we go farther?"

They stood thinking for several minutes before Dawson spoke again. "There's something else. One of the scents. I know it."

"From town?"

"No..." Dawson started but was interrupted by a low menacing growl.

Gray moved without even having to think about it. He jumped in front of Dawson, shifted and blocked him from the wolf slowly approaching from a ledge just overhead.

The dark wolf was bigger than Gray, but he had no doubt he could handle him. That was until another growl reached him from behind. He felt the disturbance in the wind as Dawson shifted into his feline form and the two of them backed up against each other.

Gray watched as they were stalked. The muscles in his legs flexed as he prepared to defend. He was less than ten feet from the wolf. He couldn't tell how close the other one was, but the stiffness from Dawson's body told him it wasn't far.

Gray took a deep breath. The other wolf watched him and, just as Gray prepared to jump, the larger wolf launched itself off the ledge. Gray caught the wolf in midair and they went down hard. The wolf could fight, that was for sure. Gray kept in good shape from being a cop and as protection for his Alpha, but the wolf he fought was good—very good. They nipped and bit as they rolled around. He couldn't take his eyes off his opponent but he hoped the commotion from the side was Dawson faring better than him. Gray just managed to stop himself from being pinned by teeth around his neck. He pushed off the other wolf, dragging his claws against the underbelly of the enemy. The black wolf snarled at him and had just gone for him again when a bobcat knocked into the wolf.

Dawson had come to his aid. Gray rose from the ground as Dawson backed the wolf up. Gray was just ducking in for another attack when he stopped at the loud and vicious roar of a cat.

They froze and glanced up at the feline above them. A bobcat, similar to Dawson but just a little bigger, was within striking distance.

The cat roared again before he started to shift. Gray wasn't about to let his attention waver from the threat around him but he had a real bad feeling about what he and Dawson had stumbled on.

His pressed against Dawson's side, silently letting the bobcat know that Gray had his back. He lifted his lip and snarled at the large wolf when he stepped closer to him.

"Stop!" the now naked man ordered. "Shift."

Gray glanced at Dawson, but he was staring up at the stranger frozen. He nudged his partner, asking what they should do. Did Dawson know the other shifters? He nudged Dawson harder and finally Dawson shook himself and nodded. They stepped back together to get more distance from the strangers before they started their shifts.

This was always a tricky position to be in. Shifters were vulnerable in the small amount of time the change was taking place. Gray allowed Dawson to complete his transformation before he began his.

Sweat covered his body and Gray had to fight the shakiness in his limbs from back-to-back transformations. He'd been in worse situations before, but Gray hated any sort of weakness.

The two shifters they had fought were back to human just as Gray and Dawson finished. Gray glanced over the others, warily pleased they didn't seem in much better shape. The wolf he'd fought was a big guy – huge and muscular with tattoos down both arms, his chest and abdomen. The big *Semper Fi* tat over his heart was testament to where he had received his training. The one who Dawson had taken on was about Gray's size, clean-cut, with the appearance of a typical soldier. Then he took in the guy still on the ledge above them. He was tall but thinner than his partners, though still muscular, and his demeanor screamed *leader*.

"Dawson," the man greeted and jumped down, landing gracefully on his feet.

Dawson had once again gone tense beside Gray. "Casey."

Gray watched the interaction. Casey moved slowly toward them and Gray didn't like the way Dawson started to shake. Gray shuffled his feet and tried to make himself bigger to block Dawson.

The man heading for them put up his hands. "Dawson…"

Gray was unprepared for Dawson coming around him then punching the guy. The stranger's head snapped back. Before he recovered, Dawson hit him again. Gray grabbed Dawson's arms and pulled him back as the other two men started forward. But the guy he'd assaulted held up a hand.

"It's okay."

Dawson didn't even try to break free of Gray's hold. Instead he stood there, breathing hard and glaring daggers at the other man.

"I know what you must think…"

"Save it, Case," Dawson snapped. "I'm all right, Gray. You can let go."

Gray still wasn't sure but he dropped his hold anyway. Dawson did seem to be in control even if he was shaking with anger.

Dawson straightened. "You all have just assaulted an officer of this county and his consultant. I would like an explanation before I haul all your asses in to jail."

The two wolves bristled before they were waved off. "RJ, Mike – please meet my brother, Dawson." Then he walked toward Gray and held out a hand. "Casey Williams."

Gray cut his eyes to Dawson, who barely nodded his confirmation. Gray shook hands, noticing the power of the cat close to the surface. "Gray Mason."

"Ah, the Wolf Council's representative," Casey said with a smile. "Didn't think you'd get here so quick."

Gray stiffened, but Casey just grinned.

"Follow us. I think we have some explaining to do," Casey stated. He strolled off before Gray could anything else.

A big part of Gray wanted to refuse just to be difficult, but Dawson sighed and followed his brother. With a shake of his head, Gray walked behind Dawson. Was this some sort of family drama or was Casey somehow involved in Gray's investigation?

Gray really hoped he wouldn't have to arrest Beth's oldest brother, but Casey's words had been suspicious.

Chapter Three

Casey led the way back up into the canyon. Dawson and Gray walked side by side, with the two wolves bringing up the rear. Gray didn't like strange wolves at his back and he stayed on alert. He needed to know what was going on. They obviously knew who he was.

The path was well hidden. He and Dawson probably would have found it but only in shifted form and by scent. Casey called out as they approached a cave entrance. A small but sturdy man edged out.

Dawson and Gray both took fighting stances and prepared to shift. It was going to suck if he had to go through another transformation, but Gray would be prepared.

"Stop." The power behind that voice had everyone freezing. "We are not enemies."

Gray gasped when the person belonging to the voice walked out of the darkness. After months of searching, he now stood face to face with Prince Zachary, the leader of the felines.

"Fuck," Dawson muttered.

"What the hell!" Gray said. He had been away from home for months in hopes that they would be able to rescue the Prince and stop a war between the two species and now the damn Prince actually stepped out of a cave of his own free will? *Maybe I won't be stopping a war after all. I might just be the one to fucking start one.* He found himself growling and couldn't have cared less whether or not the Prince was offended.

"Grayson." Prince Zachary bowed his head in respect. That actually took some of Gray's anger away. The Prince held a bundle of cloth and when he started tossing them around to the naked shifters Gray realized they were sweatpants. Even he and Dawson were thrown a pair.

Thankful for the covering, Gray quickly tugged on the worn cotton.

"We have much to speak about. Please come sit with us," Zachary requested.

Gray's feet started to move before he had even realized it. It was a shock just how much command the Prince had. He felt a little better with Dawson at his back. The Prince motioned them to the pallets of bedding on the cave floor. Gray sat warily and noted the Prince eyeing Dawson. "Dawson Williams." He held out a hand.

Dawson looked uncomfortable but grasped the Prince's hand. He let out a small unmanly squeak when he was pulled into the arms of the Prince.

"I have wanted to meet you for so long. Your brother has told me stories of this canyon and your family for many years. Forgive me, but I feel like I already know you."

Dawson cut his gaze to his brother. Casey shifted a little on his feet. It was interesting, this family dynamic, but Gray was getting impatient. He wanted to know what was going on and he wanted to know *why*. Prince Zachary released Dawson, who sat down quickly next to Gray. Gray gripped his shoulder to show support while the others nodded. Dawson nodded back in thanks.

"Before you is RJ Cross, Mike Jackson" — he motioned to the two wolves — "and Craig Grimes." He waved his hand at the small feline shifter, who was still eyeing them.

"Also let me convey my great appreciation to the Wolf Council for everything they have done for me and my people over the last few months," Prince Zachary started.

Gray bit back mentioning just how much they had done and that finding the Prince just fine and not being held captive pissed him off.

"Until last week, I had been imprisoned by a few of my trusted advisors," Prince Zachary told them. "They would discuss the wolves' involvement in the search. They even had pictures of all of you. That was how I knew who you were."

"We were tracking Zach also and almost ran into one of your other teams. It seemed like we were getting much of the same information," Casey added.

"If you were going after the Prince, why didn't you let the team you saw know? Don't you think that would have helped with the search instead of everyone covering the same ground?" Dawson questioned. Seemed he was having a hard time keeping the bitterness out of his voice.

Casey shook his head. "We didn't know who to trust. We kept getting close, but they'd pull out and move before we got there. Someone trickling in the Intel is involved."

Gray could understand that—he really could—but that didn't help him feel less frustrated. "So instead of letting us know you had the Prince safe, you continued to run and lead us here?"

"We weren't trying to draw you in. When we went in for Zach, there were only a few guards. We want everyone responsible."

"Okay." Gray agreed with that strategy. "Why tell us now?"

"You're good," Casey complimented. "And I know I can trust Dawson."

Dawson snorted. "You don't know anything about me, Case. You left. We haven't heard from you in years."

Casey frowned and scooted closer to his brother. "I've kept an eye on you and Beth as best I could. My unit does a lot of work out of the country, and the rest of the time we protect Zach. I had people watching."

"Oh, that makes me feel so much better," Dawson drawled bitterly. "You've had people spying on me."

Casey tried to respond, but the Prince cut him off. "It's one of the reasons we're here. Anyone who knows I've been rescued will have no doubt your brother was involved. He wanted to make sure you, Beth and your son were safe—

that they didn't try to get me through you."

"Why would anyone come after us?" Dawson asked suspiciously. "None of this is making any sense."

Casey linked his fingers with the Prince's. "Because we're mates."

Gray knew he was staring but he couldn't help it. *Dawson's brother is mated with the feline Prince?* He hadn't seen that one coming. As far as the Alpha Council knew, the Prince had no mate on file.

"You've got to be kidding me!" Dawson jumped to his feet.

Casey rose and crossed his arms over his chest. "He's my mate."

Dawson shook his head and looked over at Gray. "This is nuts."

Gray climbed up. "Makes sense, though." He glanced over at Casey. "That's why you kept getting close. You could feel him through your bond."

Casey nodded. "I was on a mission when he was taken. Only a few people knew that we" — he waved indicating the group around him — "weren't in the residence. I knew it had to be someone we trusted behind the kidnapping."

"Who was it?"

It was the Prince who answered. "My cousin Raphael. He was one of my advisors."

"Dawson, come on, man. We need to hear the rest of this." Gray tugged Dawson back to sitting down. He noticed that when Casey sat, it was closer to the Prince.

"I mean no disrespect to you, Prince Zachary, but this is just a lot to take in. If you're mated to Casey, that means my sister and son really are in danger."

"They are being protected. I have an old major who used to be in the unit looking out for them," Casey assured his brother. "He has been for a while now."

"What? Who?"

Casey smiled. "Claude."

"From the inn?" Gray had to ask. He'd felt the power and

44

strength from the man. "He's not a wolf or a feline." He glanced at Dawson for confirmation.

The tattooed wolf, who had until then remained quiet, chuckled. Gray glared at him. He already didn't like the guy and didn't appreciate whatever the asshole found amusing.

"Hey, it's okay, man. I never could figure it out. Finally, right before our last tour together, I asked him."

"Well…?" Gray prompted when the man didn't continue. He found that both he and Dawson were leaning forward.

RJ smiled in return.

"RJ!" Casey snapped.

The wolf RJ laughed again. "He's a hawk shifter."

"Hawk, like a bird?" Dawson scoffed. "No way."

RJ nodded. "I swear."

"Huh, that's interesting," Dawson noted but waved a hand at his brother. "But it's still beside the point. You put your family in danger. It might not matter to *you*, but *I* do have Beth and Julian to protect, whether you sent someone to watch over them or not."

"I care. I've always cared," Casey told him quietly.

Dawson obviously wasn't buying it.

"If I followed your trail here, what's to say the others won't? Why not just come out in the open and tell everyone what happened?" Gray questioned, trying to get them back on track. Maybe it was a good thing he'd never had any siblings.

"You were closer to finding Zach than anyone else. We left the maps, hoping someone on our side would pick up on them. But we didn't want it to be so obvious. Just didn't think you'd be so damn quick," Casey told them.

"We've been keeping watch. We think the cats will come in through the canyon," RJ added.

"That means they have to go through the tourists and park rangers." Dawson shook his head. "That would be stupid."

"The alternative is going through Coyote Bluff where you are. And if they're following the wolves, they know

45

Grayson is there, too," Prince Zachary reasoned.

Gray thought about it. They really were right. Anyone going back after the Prince would fare better traveling through humans than an entire town of shifters. "What's the plan? I'm assuming you have one and want our help?"

The smaller man that had been guarding the Prince grinned. "Lie in wait."

"That's it?" Dawson practically yelled. "That's your great plan?"

"This is the best military unit in the world. Every one of us is a shifter and specializes in some kind of warfare. I'm pretty sure we can take care of a few untrained cats," RJ snapped.

All the felines around the cave growled.

"You know what I mean!" RJ insisted, but he leaned away from them all.

"An entire unit of shifters?" Gray asked, curious. "Was that done on purpose?"

The men all shared a meaningful glance before Casey answered, "Yes. You know the Alpha Council and the Prince's advisors have spoken to government officials about the shifters going public?"

Gray and Dawson nodded.

"They had to have found out about us some way. Shifters have been serving in the military for hundreds of years. It doesn't take much brainpower to figure out some of us are harder to kill."

"Yeah, but..." Gray had a thousand questions. He wondered if his Alpha or their friends knew.

"There were many bad years back fifty years or so. Shifter soldiers were taken and experimented on. Zach's family was a huge part of stopping that," Casey told them proudly. "Instead, the royal family worked out a deal with the government. The shifters would continue to join the military, with the government guaranteeing their identities would remain secret. They would be able to take on missions that were not safe for the regular humans. Ones that were guaranteed to kill humans, the shifters could take and survive. The government recruited specific species with the approval of the royal family."

Gray sat in shocked silence, trying to take it all in. "If they already know all about us, then why are we even planning on going public?" Gray questioned.

"While the governments, here and in many other countries, are aware of our existence, that does not protect shifters from those who don't know about us. We can have laws to control hunting, but I still lose thousands of my species a year. In some states, if you see a cougar or even a bobcat, it's lawful to shoot right away. There must be something done about this. I'm losing too many children all too often," Prince Zachary informed him.

Gray nodded. It was the same thing Tony had always told him. But there were some missing pieces of this story. Tony had planned on approaching the Prince in the hope that Zachary would join their mission. According to the Prince, he was already known to many government officials. The lack of communication between species was a pain in the ass.

"So if you're already involved with the government and okay with being out to the public, why did your cousin kidnap you?" Dawson wondered.

"When this all comes out, there is a good chance that the military missions will also be exposed. The credit to end the torture of the shifters will go to the royal family," Prince Zachary informed them. "My cousin wants that credit."

"You don't?" Dawson asked with a raised brow in disbelief.

"No." The Prince stroked a hand down Casey's back. "I would prefer to keep the military missions a secret. To protect the ones I love."

Dawson looked away from the Prince and his brother, but Gray thought it was kind of nice. Man or woman, a mate was a mate. Wolves mated for life, so it was very sacred for them. He knew not all felines did the same, but he could almost feel it in his bones that Prince Zachary and Casey would be together for life. He'd love to hear their story someday. Hopefully relaxing with a cold beer and not hidden in a hot and stuffy cave.

"What can we do to help? I'm sorry, but I do need to tell my Alpha and the other teams to stop searching. They're away from their Pack and families. It is starting to take a toll on everyone."

"I understand, but I have to ask you to tell only your Alpha for now, if you're sure you can trust him," Prince Zachary requested. "I believe he can be trusted, but my cousin is working with some wolves. The only way to ensure we capture everyone involved this time is by keeping our plans just between us."

Gray nodded. "I can do that. As long as I can speak with Tyler about it, I agree to keep all of this under wraps."

"What about the sheriff?" Dawson enquired.

"One of the reasons I picked the canyon was because of Joe. If this went wrong, I was going to contact him," Casey admitted.

"I think we should bring in the sheriff," Dawson told his brother. "In the long run, it will be better to have his support. I know you all think you can handle this, but them just being able to get to the Prince speaks volumes on how organized these guys are."

The military men all exchanged glances before they eventually nodded.

"You'll take care of that for us?" Casey asked. "We can't risk taking Zachary into town yet and I won't leave him here unprotected."

Zachary snorted. "He acts like I can't take care of myself."

"Hello!" Casey waved his hand over Zachary. "Kidnapped!"

"I wasn't expecting an attack in my own damn bedroom," Zachary declared. To Gray it appeared to be a familiar argument. Which it probably was, considering that Casey had just gotten his mate back and was probably on an emotional high.

"We'll head into town and talk with Joe. See if we can get any reports from the rangers," Dawson said.

"We have no way to communicate with you, though," Gray observed.

RJ stood and walked over to his backpack. He pulled out a handheld radio and passed it over to Gray. "Use channel eight. It's as secure as we can make it with the technology we brought with us."

Gray accepted the radio and nodded. "We won't contact you unless we encounter any problems. But how about we take a run tonight and meet back up about midnight?" He still thought there was something wrong with the other wolf, but this was about a bigger issue. Finding those responsible for the kidnapping of the Prince and ending the entire ordeal.

RJ nodded. "Two wolves won't cause too much suspicion, even if we are being watched."

Gray stood. "Then we have a busy night ahead of us."

The other men dipped their heads in goodbye as Casey stood to walk them to the front of the cave.

"I'll give you a minute," Gray told Dawson, clipping him on the shoulder. He strolled back into the sunlight, glad to get out in the open. He didn't like the closed-in feeling. Natural wolves might make a den in a cave similar to that, but he preferred the freedom to be able to run.

Dawson and Casey spoke in low but urgent tones and Gray did his best to ignore them. Not easy with his sharpened senses, so he ambled farther away, humming low to himself. Dawson followed him a couple of minutes later. He was shaking his head and mumbling.

"You okay?" Gray asked his new friend.

Dawson glanced up and offered a small smile. "On one hand, I'm relieved to see him again. I know Beth will be thrilled beyond words. But on the other hand, he was close by and didn't contact me, put my family in danger and has a whole other life I know nothing about. I'm angry...and just a little impressed by him."

"I bet that punch felt good, though."

Dawson laughed like Gray had intended. "It did. Really good. But he better watch out—Beth has quite a left hook herself."

The mention of the pretty feline had Gray's body responding. He merely grunted trying to not give any away of his thoughts from earlier.

"You want to talk about it?" Dawson enquired as they jumped down an opening in the canyon.

"About?" Gray asked, distracted by his thoughts of Beth.

"Look, Gray." Dawson stopped walking. "I know my sister. That little display of nerves this morning at the inn is not like her. She's confident, smart and at ease with everyone. Something about you made her nervous."

Gray exhaled. "She makes me nervous, too."

Dawson threw back his head and cackled.

"Not funny," Gray grumbled and started to walk again.

Dawson caught up with him and slung an arm over his shoulder. "Come on, man—it's funny! The big bad detective wolf is nervous about the little bobcat?"

"It's not her animal that makes me uneasy and you know it. One of my best friends just found her mate. I didn't think Kiley would ever mate with anyone. We'd... We'd spent some time together, but it just never felt destined..." Gray tried to explain.

"You couldn't force it, because it just wasn't there. There was someone else for her," Dawson finished.

Gray shrugged. "Pretty much. But it had me wondering if there was someone waiting for me, too. I thought about it a lot while I've been on my own these last few months. Now I'm not sure if these feelings I have..." Gray hesitated. "If I just want it so bad, I'm reading more into the attraction than I should. And it's weird discussing this with her brother. Especially because we're both still half-naked."

Dawson nudged him to a stop. "Just be honest with her. Like I said, Beth is smart. I have to believe it will work out. One way or the other. Just take things slow and see. I don't want her hurt. It would kill me." Dawson glared. "Remember that. But I want her happy."

Gray patted his shoulder. "We have time to figure it out. Or at least I think we do. I don't think that my Alpha will want me out of here. If the Prince is requesting our help, Tyler will probably be okay with me sticking around a little longer."

"And if he decides to send you home?"

"He won't," Gray assured him.

Dawson lifted a brow.

"Tyler's my Alpha, but he's also my friend. He listens to me and will respect my opinion. If I want to stay, he won't have a problem with it."

"Good." Dawson motioned ahead. "Then let's hit the road. I think you have a date tonight. With two chaperones."

Gray groaned good-naturedly but trailed after him.

* * * *

Beth watched Julian as he played in the front yard. She'd seen her brother and Gray pull up earlier. The wolf shifter had waved before heading into the hotel. She'd asked how it had gone when Dawson had passed her going into the house, but he'd shaken his head and told her it was complicated.

She wasn't sure what that meant but she hoped the two men had gotten along. She'd spent the day thinking about what had happened the night before. She could admit that the strong feelings she'd had for Gray from the beginning meant something. And she was determined to see where they might lead. Gray might only be there for a little while, but they owed it to themselves to explore what was going on between them.

"Don't climb on the dog house," she called to Julian.

The little boy grinned and waved, heading toward the swing set Dawson had built.

"I swear, he's a monkey instead of a bobcat," Dawson voiced behind her.

She chuckled. "I agree." He came up beside her and she leaned a little into him.

"There is something I need to talk to you about," her brother announced softly.

Beth spun around to give him her attention. Dawson was open with her about everything except his work. Her brother had told her numerous times that it was his job to make the world safe for her and Julian. Beth might get frustrated sometimes, but she also liked the fact that someone thought she was important enough to protect.

He motioned to the porch and they both sat on the swing. Julian was far enough away that he wouldn't overhear their conversation as he played. "We found more today than we thought."

"About the Prince?"

Dawson took her hand in his. "We *found* the Prince."

Beth gasped. "That's wonderful! Why didn't you say something earlier?"

"He'd already been rescued. The trail they left was supposed to bring the kidnappers into a trap. Gray just beat them there."

"You don't think Gray's involved, do you?" She didn't want to think that way about the other man.

"No, no way," Dawson said adamantly. "But with them hiding in the canyon, I'm worried about the repercussions for the town."

Beth could see where he was coming from. "So they're up there hiding and just waiting for the men who captured the Prince once before to come after him again? What if they decide to come into Coyote Bluff first?"

"That's a concern, but I don't really think they'll try to travel through here. That doesn't make me feel any better though, because if they do, both you and Julian are in danger."

"Us? I doubt anyone will bother us," Beth tried to assure

her brother. *Why would they bother with two bobcats?*

"They might if they know a member of the rescue team is your brother," Dawson told her quietly.

Beth frowned. "How would…?"

"Crap, Beth! Casey was there!" he finally blurted out.

She inhaled sharply. "Casey is here?" *My oldest brother is a couple of miles away and Dawson has seen him?* "Why didn't he call? Or come by the house? Does he not want to see us?"

"No, I don't think that's it at all. He was actually trying to protect you."

"Protect?" she repeated. "By hiding out near our home?"

Her brother chuckled. "Yeah, I don't really get his reasoning, either, but I think that deep down he just wanted to be here. He's using the excuse of knowing the canyons as a reason to come home." Dawson wrapped an arm around her shoulder. "He said he's been keeping an eye on us."

"That doesn't really make me feel better."

"I said the same thing," Dawson said. "God, Beth, this whole fucking thing is a mess. I can't believe this afternoon even happened. It feels fucking surreal."

"He's okay, though?" she asked. Why she cared about a man who couldn't even bother to call home and talk to her she didn't know, but she did.

"He's fine. More than I'd say. I even met his mate."

"*Casey's mated?*" For some reason she'd always pictured her oldest brother living off the land as some kind of survivalist or something. She'd never really thought about him starting a family. "What's she like?"

Dawson's grin was wide and wicked. "Our brother is mated to the Prince of Felines."

"Maybe you should start from the beginning," Beth said, stunned. "The very beginning."

* * * *

Thirty minutes later Beth stepped into the inn's dining room ahead of Dawson and Julian, still reeling from what her brother had told her. Military units, kidnapping, mates… It was all so much to take in.

She spotted Gray already seated at a table set for four. He noticed her and stood, smiling. She gulped. *Wow, he is an attractive man.* This was exactly what she needed to take her mind off the family drama that she'd found herself in. Gray was the perfect distraction. Everything she had learned about him spoke to how dedicated he'd been to finding the Prince. Not many people would have done that for a stranger. She didn't know any other shifters who would have sacrificed so much for another species.

"Wolf!" Julian cried and raced around her.

Gray laughed as he hefted Julian up in the air.

Dawson was shaking his head as they reached Gray and Julian. "Julian, what have I told you about not calling people by their name?"

Julian stuck his lip out. "Sorry, Dad."

All the adults were smiling as the party of four sat at the table. Beth found her gaze trapped in Gray's as he took his seat next to her. He leaned in and her breath caught.

"I'm glad you came," he whispered.

She bobbed her head up and down. She was happy as well. She'd wanted to go out and hunt her oldest brother down to demand answers, but Dawson had talked her out of it.

"Maybe after dinner we can take that walk," he offered.

"Su…sure."

"Why are you whispering?" Julian asked loudly from Gray's other side.

He straightened and winked at her. "I'm sorry, Julian. Whispering is rude. And what did you do today, young man?"

Julian grinned widely and launched into a story about how he and his best buddy Jamey had wanted to learn how to fly, but Aunt Beth wouldn't let them borrow sheets for a parachute. Dorothy came over to take their orders and everyone chose the night's special of meat loaf and mashed potatoes, except for Julian, who wanted Claude's chicken fingers – the 'best chicken fingers in the world'.

"Did you call your Alpha?" Dawson enquired across the table.

Gray cut his glance to Beth and Julian.

Dawson just nodded.

"Yeah, Tyler agreed to keep it under wraps but wants to call in a couple more wolves for protection. He doesn't want it to come down on the community here."

Beth smiled. She liked that everyone was worried about the residents. She still couldn't believe that her older brother was so close after so many years.

"I told him I wanted to stay here and see this through." Gray glanced at her. "That I had a few things I needed to see to." Gray blushed as he said it.

Beth bit back a giggle. It was quite cute. "Good," she approved, nudging his foot under the table.

Gray beamed and leaned back in his chair.

The rest of dinner went smoothly. Beth found herself leaning in and losing herself in the conversation about Gray's Pack and friends. But even though he laughed and told stories, she could catch the impression that Gray wasn't one hundred percent happy. The stories were always about others in his Pack. What he had witnessed. And a longing in his voice told her he was missing something. She wondered if he even realized it.

The dinner dishes were cleared away and Julian got a plate full of cookies with a glass of milk while the adults decided on coffee. Claude walked into the dining room and waved at them.

"Will you excuse me for a minute?" Dawson asked, pushing away from the table.

Dawson motioned to the outer room and Claude nodded.

"I wonder what that's about?" Beth wondered out loud.

Gray didn't answer, just picked up his coffee. She got the feeling he knew, though. She would ask Dawson later.

"You haven't been downtown, have you? We have a

beautiful pond and garden," she mentioned to Gray, wanting to share it with him.

"No, not yet. I haven't actually seen anything but the inn and the canyons."

"Don't you just love it here though?" Julian questioned. "When I get big I'm gonna work here with Claude. Or maybe with my dad." He tilted his head. "Or maybe I'm gonna be a teacher. But I still want to fly, too."

"I have no doubt you can do whatever you want," Dawson said to the boy. He winked at Beth. "Maybe do all of those things."

"Yeah," Julian bounced in his seat. "I'll do all of them."

Dawson interrupted, coming back to the table. "Julian, you ready to go home? It's almost bedtime."

Julian groaned dramatically but jumped up into his dad's arms when they were offered.

Dawson glanced her way. "Coming, Beth?" He smirked at her because he already knew her plan to spend time with Gray. He'd also given her a few vague comments that she took as his approval of her and Gray. Not that she needed her brother's permission, but Dawson meant the world to her and she was happy that he seemed to really like Gray.

"Actually, I'm going to show Gray around a little."

Gray stood and held out a hand. "I'll call you later and we'll discuss our plans for tomorrow."

They shook and her brother peeked over at her. "Be careful."

She watched her brother and nephew leave the dining room before turning back to Gray. "You ready?"

They walked silently through the inn until they were outside. Beth took a deep breath once out in the warm air. She loved the Texas nights. Still warm enough to do anything without having to worry about a lot of rain or bad weather. Even in winter, the lowest lows were only forty degrees.

"You love it here," Gray observed from beside her.

Beth hadn't realized she'd closed her eyes but opened

them and looked up. "I really do. Let me show you why."

They walked side by side down the drive onto the main road. "The canyons give us the privacy to shift and with so many different species, we have enough space to keep everyone happy."

"I've almost always shifted in forests," Gray admitted. "Since I've been on the road it's been hard to find places, but I have to admit the canyon holds its own beauty."

She sighed happily and entwined her arm around his, glad that he saw a little of what she did. Beth pointed out all the attractions the community had to offer as she led him to the middle of town. Gray asked questions and commented as they slowly made their way.

When they were just outside the gardens, Gray paused. "Wow!"

Beth had to agree. She loved this area. She could smell the flowers for miles with her shifter-heightened senses. On a night like this, with the soft breeze, it was probably even farther. Beth took Gray's hand and tugged him under the arch into the circle. He gazed at everything and continued to take deep breaths. She let him just enjoy the sight and smells for a while.

Finally he rotated and cupped her face. "Thank you for sharing this with me."

He leaned in slowly as if to give her time to pull away. She didn't want to, though. Instead, she stretched up to her toes and closed the distance. Gray's lips were moist and the kiss was strong without being forceful. She tilted her head and opened to give him access. He moved his hands from her face and embraced her.

She moaned at the solid embrace, loving the way he surrounded her.

"Beth," he panted out as they paused to catch their breath.

"Yes," she hissed, taking his mouth again. Pure heat this time. While the first kiss had been sweet and romantic, now she attacked his mouth, pouring all the passion she felt into him. He groaned and she swallowed the sound. Wrapping her legs around his waist when he lifted her up, she pressed intimately against him.

"God, Beth," he murmured against her skin, mouthing down her neck. She arched, pressing her pussy harder into his cock. "We shouldn't be doing this."

He was hard and she wanted to feel him. "I want you," she told him, starting to rock. It felt so good. He was solid against her and if she didn't get him inside her, she felt as though she would explode. It wasn't as if she was a slut or anything. There was just something about this one man that called to everything inside her. Besides, with the Prince found, she didn't have much time with Gray. He would be leaving very soon. Beth wanted to have a piece of him to remember after she was left all alone once again.

"Can't... We can't here," he disputed even as he continued to explore her, his hand under her shirt kneading her breast.

Oh, they could and would. Beth wasn't one for public displays but she did know of a private place. Excitement rushed through her as she took the biggest chance of her life. "This way! Come here." She dropped her legs to the ground and grabbed his hand. She tugged him farther into the garden to a private stretch of grass. Once she knew they were hidden by the bushes, she nudged him back.

He dropped to the ground, taking her with him to sit on his lap. She grasped his neck and kissed him again. He had both his hands under her shirt now, smoothing it up and off. The warm night air caused goosebumps to break out on her.

"From the moment I saw you I couldn't believe how beautiful you were." Gray spoke while cupping her breasts. She arched her back, pushing into his hands. "I need to taste you."

"Yes..." she moaned while he laid her back. The grass was damp but she didn't mind. Especially when he swept aside the cotton bra she wore and closed his lips over her taut nipple.

She whimpered—it felt so good. *Too* good.

"God, your skin," he marveled, moving to her other breast and nipple. He teased, tormented and lavished attention upon her while she cried out in ecstasy.

"Please... Please," she begged, needing more.

He worked his fingers into the opening of her jeans while he stimulated her with his mouth as he moved down her body. She grabbed at the back of his head, holding on to him as best she could. He unsnapped her jeans and lowered the zipper and she lifted her hips to help push them down.

His eyes met hers and she could see the heat and passion. "Tell me you want this, Beth. That it's okay. I'll stop now, but I want to taste you."

She had to take deep breaths to calm herself.

"Tell me this is more than just lust. That in the morning you won't regret that I'm a wolf."

It was on the tip of her tongue to tease him, but when she saw the flash of insecurity in his eyes she stopped in time. She caressed his head before cupping his jaw. "I know who you are, Grayson. I want you."

He nodded. "Thank God!"

She shrieked when he yanked her pants the rest of the way down and closed his mouth over the thin cotton of her panties. Even with the flimsy barrier, his mouth was hot. She dug her heels into the dirt under her.

"Your smell..." He groaned. "Got to taste." He snapped the edges of her panties easily and inhaled deeply. The first lick was just a tease.

"Gray... Gray..."

He growled and held her hips.

Beth actually screamed when he opened her and started to feast. "Oh, my —"

He used his tongue to ease inside her, his lips to suck her clit and his fingers to tease everywhere.

"More... Please more," she pleaded.

Gray gave it to her, licking and nibbling as he brought her closer to the edge. Hands under her ass, he tilted her hips and ate at her. Finally it grew to be too much. She wanted to hold out, to wait until he was buried inside her, but she couldn't. She raked her nails into the ground and shook as she finally climaxed. Gray licked her clean even as she started to work at his shoulders to move him up. He lifted his head and grinned the perfect big-bad-wolf grin.

She drew him up into her arms so they could kiss. She could taste herself on his tongue, but more, she felt his erection bulging. Beth cupped him through his jeans and he bucked while moaning. "You're so hard for me."

"I am."

"Good." She worked his jeans open and down before closing a hand around his hard shaft. She pumped him a few times while he rocked against her hold. As good as he felt in her hand, she wanted to feel him stretching her.

"Make love to me," she demanded, giving him some rough pulls.

He grunted and kissed her hard. She knew she had him.

"I want to see you," he commanded, settling between her legs. "Keep your eyes open, watch me and feel me."

She tried her best as he gently began to push in. He'd already used his tongue and fingers to open her so, while he fitted snugly, she had to close her eyes at just how right it felt.

"Beth," he coaxed, slipping out and sliding back inside.

She lifted her head and their eyes locked. He thrust back in harder and deeper. She remained entranced until he let go of his control. Breaking eye contact, he threw his head back and started to plow into her, each masterful stroke deep and claiming, letting her know that he owned every inch of her. She lifted her hips and met each frenzied plunge as they drove to the edge of desire.

Before she even realized she was ready, she felt the tingle inside. Her back bowed and she called his name as he guided her into her second orgasm of the night. She clutched at him as he rode her through her climax until he finally cried out and pumped his seed inside her.

Their ragged breaths mixed as he leaned his forehead

against hers. That was unquestionably the best sexual encounter she'd had in her life. She held him to her tightly. He mumbled something so she loosened her grip. "What?"

He laughed breathlessly, still not fully recovered. "I said you have to come back to my room with me. We have to do that again."

Dropping her head back, she snickered. "That's the best idea I've heard in years."

Chapter Four

Gray didn't want to leave Beth — she felt so good tucked close to his side, her hair fanned out against the white pillowcase. He pressed a soft kiss to the side of her neck before admiring her for another moment. He hadn't planned for the night to go quite like it had. Not that he would complain. She'd been embarrassed on the walk back to the inn and he had found it sweet.

After assuring him over and over that she never did things like that, Gray had had to kiss her into silence. That had almost led to another public display, but he'd managed to get control of himself. Still, the night had taken a surprising and fucking amazing turn of events.

He'd been hoping for a nice quiet walk and maybe to be able to sneak a kiss or two. He'd wanted to woo Beth like she deserved. The walk had been wonderful, but when he'd seen her in the garden, moonlight behind her, he just hadn't been able to control himself. The first kiss had done him in.

He had no doubt he wasn't reading deeper into his feelings. Beth Williams was the woman for him. Now the real issues would start. Gray didn't care that she was a feline. He'd questioned her earlier, making sure she understood what he was. But now would come the backlash of what everyone else thought. There'd never been talk of mating across species. Not that he was ready to mate, but eventually he could see himself settling down with her.

They needed to spend more time together first. He was sure that Tyler would give him some vacation time that he'd most definitely earned by being away on this latest assignment. The police department that he served would just have to deal with their number one detective being gone longer.

Gray wasn't ready to move to Coyote Bluff, but he and Beth were going to have to come up with a way to continue their relationship.

The biggest obstacle was the distance they lived from each other, but he'd think of something.

He slipped out of bed as quietly as he could. There was just enough time to shift and get to his meeting. Gray pulled on a pair of jeans and a T-shirt before grabbing his shoes. The door clicked softly as he closed it behind him, and he had to fight the urge to go back and kiss Beth one more time.

Shaking his head at himself, he made his way through the inn, remaining silent so he wouldn't wake anyone else up. He used the back door to leave and immediately caught the feline scent. He crouched, dropped his shoes, a growl rumbling in his throat.

"Easy, wolf." Casey Williams stepped out of the shadows.

Gray straightened and crossed his arms over his chest. "What are you doing here?"

"I wanted to… I had to see for myself they were okay." Casey shrugged and walked up the steps.

Gray relaxed. He could smell the sincerity from the bobcat. "They're okay."

Casey nodded to the porch furniture. Gray took a seat first. Casey passed by him to lean against the rail before stiffening. He took a deep breath and hissed. "You've been with my sister," he accused.

Shit, he really should have showered but he hadn't wanted to leave Beth. Besides, he'd thought he was meeting RJ and hadn't thought Beth's scent would be an issue. Gray held up both hands. "It's not what you think."

But Casey wasn't listening. He snarled and took a step toward Gray. Gray had jumped to his feet to defend himself when the back door slammed closed.

"Casey Williams, don't you touch him!"

Both men froze as Beth stepped away from the door.

"Beth," Casey murmured her name. He appeared both shocked and almost desperate to reach for her.

She smiled, her entire face lighting up, and held out her arms. "Hello, big brother."

Casey moved quickly, pulling her into a tight embrace and rocking her back and forth. Gray felt like an intruder witnessing such an emotional display. But he was happy for both of them too.

Casey drew back and cupped her cheeks. "You are so beautiful."

She laughed. "You're not too bad yourself."

He hugged her again before letting her go and glancing over at Gray. "Maybe we can talk later. I need to discuss something with Gray."

She shook her head and patted his chest. "Nice try. You and Gray can talk about what's going on with the Prince in front of me. However, you will not discuss my relationship with Gray."

"Wow," Gray murmured. He was sort of in awe of Beth at the moment.

"Your 'relationship'? He's been here two days and you have a 'relationship'?" Casey asked.

Casey's tone agitated Gray enough that he started to growl. Beth pulled him back to the furniture. "Down, boys. Casey, you don't get to question anything I do with Gray or anyone else for that matter. You weren't here before and, while I'm glad you're back, I am an adult."

Gray had started to grin at her show of independence from her brother until she'd mentioned someone else. Was there someone else? He hadn't thought to ask before. They'd just met and...

Beth slapped his chest. "Knock it off. There is no one else."

Gray blushed at being caught.

Casey moved back to lean against the rail again. "Sorry, but you are still my sister. Family has to look out for one another."

"Great!" Beth said cheerfully. "I'd love to meet the Prince and ask him why, if he knew about us, he never came to see us. I mean, even if you were out of the country, he still could have called or let us know you were still alive. Or, you know...tell us he mated you."

Casey had the grace to drop his head. "I am sorry about that. I kept meaning to get hold of you all. But every time I came close, something would happen and I felt...knew it would be safer if you didn't have any contact from me."

Beth snorted. "You keep thinking that, Case. In the meantime, you have no say about me and Gray."

Casey nodded while frowning. Gray didn't think that would be the end of the subject, though.

"Now, if you guys would like to discuss what dragged Gray out of bed at almost midnight, I'm all ears."

Obviously Casey wasn't going to be able to keep her out of the discussion any more than Gray was. With a heavy sigh, Casey waved his hand at Gray to start.

"Joe wasn't happy that you didn't let him know what was going on. I think he'll have a few words with you when he sees you," Gray told him, just a little amused. "But he agreed that he needed to add support to make sure no one got away and nothing was left to chance."

"We can handle this," Casey argued. "We have been doing this kind of stuff for years."

"But he has to protect his community, too."

Casey ran his hands roughly over his face. "I know. I just didn't think it would be so complicated."

"Someone kidnapped the Prince. That's pretty damned complicated already," Beth piped up.

Both men glared at her. She ducked her head, smirking,

"Anyway," Casey restarted, "I really thought they would come after Zach and it would be done. Over fifty people entered the canyon today. Seven of those stayed to camp and didn't leave. I don't know if they took the bait or not."

"Maybe they decided to come in like we did," Gray suggested.

"Claude's had some guys watching the town limits. No one entered who he didn't know except you."

"So we don't know any more than this morning?" Gray questioned, even though he knew the answer.

"It's frustrating," Casey shared. "I just want this over with. We decided our last mission was it. We're ready to get out. I want to spend time with my family. RJ's brother just accepted a position as Alpha and has asked him to come home. Craig will stay with the Prince as his personal guard after all of this. And Mike... I'm not sure what Mike's plans are, but he says he's tired of fighting for everyone else."

Gray could understand. The men had lost a lot of time serving.

"There are other members of the team, but us four started together and want to finish together. I trust those men with my life...with my mate's life."

"Everyone needs help. I might not have ever served in the military, but no matter how good you all are, there are still people who can take some of the pressure off. That way you can spend time with your family," Gray offered.

Beth took his hand and squeezed it gently. "Let us help you, Casey."

"Yes, I know," he conceded. "I'm just not used to having civilians involved. Or sisters."

Beth just beamed at him.

Gray chuckled.

"RJ and Mike are doing a sweep of the canyon tonight. Trying to pick up any scents that don't belong." He glanced to Gray. "I know you were supposed to run with RJ, but I had to come to town."

"You're sure you weren't followed? No one caught sight of you?" Gray asked.

"I'm sure." Casey didn't seem annoyed by the question. "Just as I'm sure that Claude is watching us from an upstairs window even now."

Gray glanced around but still didn't spot the hawk shifter.

Casey chuckled. "You won't see him if he doesn't want

you to."

"I'm getting an education here on shifters, for sure," Gray commented. He'd admired the many birds of prey species but hadn't thought he'd ever get to meet one.

"That tends to happen when you come to Coyote Bluff," Beth said. "And I think it's a good thing."

Gray nodded.

"I'd better get out of here." Casey pushed himself off the rail. "We plan to stay a little longer once things are sorted out. I want to reconnect with you and Dawson. I also have years of absence to make up for with a nephew."

"That sounds good to me," Beth told him.

"The sheriff wants to head up to talk to you and the Prince first thing," Gray added.

"I'll let the others know," Casey said, stepping away from the porch.

Gray stood, bringing Beth up with him.

Gray and Casey shook hands before Casey pulled Beth in again. "It's good to see you, sis."

She hugged him tight. "Glad you're home."

Casey stepped down the porch. He disappeared back into the shadows.

Beth pivoted to Gray. "Now, why don't we discuss you leaving me in the middle of the night to meet with strange felines?"

"Now, darling," Gray drawled as best he could. "You know you're the only strange feline I would prefer meeting in the middle of the night."

She threw her arms around his neck. "Good, now take me back to bed. I need my beauty sleep."

Gray hauled her into his arms. "I'll take you back to bed, but I don't promise you'll get much sleep."

She attached her lips to his neck as he strode across the porch and in through the back door. She didn't let up on her assault even when he stumbled a couple of times.

"Don't drop me," she taunted, running her tongue into his ear.

He shivered, making his way to his room as quickly as he could while trying to not drop her for real. Once he reached his door he pushed it open, slipped inside and closed it by pressing her against it. She laughed and threw her head back.

Gray covered her mouth with his, thrusting his tongue inside and swallowing her moan. He was already hard as he rubbed against her. His body had never responded so quickly or surely before. Just another sign that she was meant for him.

She gripped his cock through his jeans and squeezed. His knees went weak and he fell forward, knocking her farther against the door.

"It's my turn," she said with promise in her voice before dropping slowly to her knees.

Gray gasped when she ran her hands up the inside seam of his pants.

"I get to taste you now," she told him, rubbing her cheek against his erection. "Tease and pleasure you."

"You don't have to..." he tried to tell her but almost swallowed his tongue when she mouthed his cock through his jeans.

"I don't have to do anything but taste you," Beth agreed. She deftly unsnapped his jeans with her slender fingers before pulling them down. "Mmm. No underwear," she purred, nudging his erect shaft with her nose. "I like."

"Damn!" he yelled when she wrapped one hand around the base of his dick and licked the head.

Beth moaned around the tip of his cock and it was all he could do not to thrust into the warm, moist haven of her mouth. "Beth, please, I'm..."

She popped off and gave him a sexy grin. "You're going to enjoy this," she assured him.

Yes, he was, but he didn't know if he would survive it. Her lips wrapped around his shaft and she swallowed him all the way down her throat. The way she used her tongue on the vein under his cockhead almost had his eyes rolling to the back of his head.

"Baby... Baby..." He fisted his hands to keep him from grabbing her hair and just pounding into her mouth. It was sweet torture, what she was doing to him.

She edged back, hollowing her cheeks and sucking.

"Jeez, oh God," he pleaded with her.

She moved her head up and down his shaft, gripping his hip with her free hand to encourage him to move. And, God help him, he had to move. He thrust shallowly at first, trying not to hurt her, but eventually he snapped and cried out, plunging his hips in time with her moving on his cock.

All too sudden, the tingling started and he knew he was going to come. He slid his fingers through her hair.

"Baby... Beth..."

She hummed and he took that as permission. Three more thrusts and he slammed his head forward into the door, biting back a howl as he released. She swallowed him down and kept sucking when he didn't go completely soft. He pulled her off his half-hard dick and up into his arms. He tasted his seed mixed with her unique flavor as he plundered her mouth. Holding her tight, he stumbled his way to the bed, still unmade from earlier. He dropped down, covering her body with his. He yanked off his shirt which they hadn't managed to remove, before attacking her clothes. She was naked and bared for him in seconds.

"You're the most amazing woman I've ever met," he told her, fingering her clit before slipping two fingers through her slick folds and opening her up.

She clawed at his back. "In me... In me..."

He growled and flipped her over. "Hands and knees! Come on, baby," he encouraged.

Beth hurried to comply, arching her back in invitation. Nipping her right ass cheek made her squeak and he chuckled. Gray ran his tongue over the small hurt. "Perfect. So perfect, honey."

She pushed back into him. He lined his cock up to her entrance and pressed in. She opened for him, squeezing tightly.

"So good," he praised, pulling out and slamming back in.

It was going to be quick. Even though he had just come, he was so out of control for this woman. He set a hard, steady pace pounding into her tight, wet pussy. His wolf was close to the surface, demanding he claim their mate. His eyes began to shift and his teeth elongated. He held the animal back and continued to hammer inside.

Beth thrust back, met each crazed stroke, urging him on. Screaming, she started to climax, the walls of her cunt clamping down almost painfully.

Gray continued to plunge deep, enjoying the loud pleased noises.

"Come inside me," she whispered.

Gray came hard, his vision darkening. He couldn't hold himself up and dropped his weight on top of her.

"You'd better not fall asleep," she murmured.

He managed a grunt.

* * * *

Morning came too early. Gray groaned at the sunlight sneaking its way into his room. He rolled his bed partner closer and buried his face in the back of her neck. Beth hummed softly, snuggling back into him. He cupped her breast and kissed down her shoulder. What would it be like to wake this way every morning? Would she get tired of him? Probably. He couldn't expect Beth to change her entire life for him.

Gray had a very important position with his Pack, but Beth had family who relied on her. He'd been thinking they'd find a way of working things out, but in the back of his mind, he'd imagined Beth joining him in Colorado.

His home was beautiful, with a gorgeous view of the mountains and a growing Pack who needed him. But how would Beth fit in with a Pack of wolf shifters? In Coyote Bluff Beth was surrounded by shifters who already accepted her.

Gray's Pack accepted him and cared for him, but he had no idea how they'd react to having a bobcat around all the time, being a part of them.

Beth rolled over and their lips met. "You're thinking awfully hard for it being such a beautiful start to the day," she said after they parted.

"Good morning." He smiled, trying to let go of his worries. At the moment he had.

"Morning." She snuggled deeper into his arms. "I slept so well last night."

So had he. Gray might not have been used to sharing his bed for more than sex, but he'd enjoyed holding Beth all night. And he wasn't sure what to do about it yet, so he kissed in her response. She responded beautifully, opening to him and allowing him to roll on top. She ran her hands down his back while he nibbled on her neck.

"Beth." He loved to say her name.

The pounding on the bedroom door startled them both. Gray glanced at the clock and noticed he was already late. "Damn it."

He kissed Beth one more time before picking up his jeans and hopping into them. More pounding. "All right, all right—keep your pants on."

He opened the door to an amused-looking Claude. "The sheriff is already downstairs and Dawson is on his way. Wanted me to make sure you were out of bed."

Beth laughed behind him. He smiled at the older man. "I'll be right down. Thanks."

Claude nodded and headed back down the hall. Gray closed the door and pointed toward the bed. "I'm late. You keep your sexy ass there while I shower. No more distracting me."

She licked her lips, causing his cock to twitch again. "Want me to wash your back?"

"No!" he growled at her. "I have to leave the room before noon."

Her happy voice followed him into the bathroom. "I'll

just entertain myself then."

He thumped his dick, trying to get himself under control, and jumped into a lukewarm shower. It was the best he could do under the time constraint.

Less than ten minutes later he was back, dressing while Beth smirked at him from the bed. He loved her playful attitude and really could see them sharing mornings like this together.

Once he was ready for the day ahead, he leaned over the bed and kissed her as chastely as he could. "Please be careful today. We don't think anyone is in town, but you never know."

Thankfully, she nodded. "Julian is probably already downstairs. We'll stay either here or at the house. We'll even stay out of town."

She must have read the relief on his face.

"Hey, I won't do anything to put Julian at risk," she promised.

"Or yourself?" he added.

She smiled shyly. "Or myself. I promise."

He kissed her again, this one deeper and a lot dirtier. His cock, which had finally settled, perked right back up.

"Trouble," he grumbled at her, pulling away and adjusting himself.

"See you later," she called and blew him a kiss.

He smiled the entire way down the stairs to the front entrance. There he met the sheriff, Dawson and Claude. Dorothy handed him a travel mug of coffee and a foil-wrapped package. *Wow, the citizens of this town really do watch out for one another.*

"For the road," she told him with a fond smile.

He dipped his head in thanks. "Appreciate it."

"You and Gray head out the same way as you did yesterday. Take the direct route. Claude and I will follow and make sure no one else is tailing you," the sheriff ordered.

"Claude?" Gray asked, becoming uneasy. He didn't want

to leave the inn unprotected.

"I have my deputy stationed here and Claude has a few friends close by. Everyone here will be safe," Joe answered his unspoken concern.

Gray nodded and followed the other men out. He slid into the passenger seat beside Dawson, taking a deep breath to get his bearings. He needed to get into the mindset of planning a mission with the felines. This was Gray's chance to finally end the entire investigation and send all of the other shifters back home to their families.

"Go ahead and eat while I drive," Dawson said. "You're going to need your energy to hike back up the canyon."

Gray didn't miss Dawson's smirk. "Got something to say?"

"Not a thing," Dawson replied with a smile. "Just thought you might be tired this morning. You know, since my sister didn't come home last night."

He moaned. "Man, I don't want to have this conversation."

"Eat!" Dawson ordered.

Gray drank his coffee and chowed down on the best breakfast burrito he'd ever had. The pepper from the sausage mixed wonderfully with the fluffy eggs. There was some sort of sauce that contained the perfect amount of heat. "I got to tell you, I could move here just for the food," he told Dawson.

"Are you thinking about it?" Dawson asked quietly.

Gray glanced over at him, not realizing how his words might be taken. "Thinking about it?" *Am I?* No, there was no way he'd leave Tyler.

"Moving here," Dawson clarified.

Gray crumpled up the foil and took a drink of his rich coffee to give him time. He knew he was stalling. So did Dawson, by the frown he gave him.

"I can't," he admitted, not glancing at the other man. "I have responsibilities at home."

"Look, Gray, I won't pressure you. Beth is a big girl and she knows what she's doing. Like I said yesterday, just be honest with her. I'm not going to go all big brother on you."

"Yeah, one of you is enough," Gray muttered.

Dawson cut his eyes to him.

"Casey stopped by last night instead of RJ. He said he wanted to see for himself that all of you were okay."

"And he caught Beth's scent on you?" Dawson guessed.

"Yes," Gray smiled. "Tried to go all protective on me, but Beth had followed me out."

"I can just imagine what she'd had to say to him," Dawson shared with a grin.

"It was interesting," Gray commented. "She's unlike anyone I've ever met. Beth was standing there, reading Casey the riot act, looking sexy as hell but still as sweet as anyone I've ever met."

"She is both fierce and kind," Dawson said.

"I'm glad I came here," Gray shared. "I don't know what's going to happen, but I will never regret meeting you all."

Dawson didn't say anything else but Gray got the feeling that his new friend understood what Gray was trying to say. They sat in comfortable silence for a few minutes and had almost reached their stop before Dawson spoke up. "With the way that things unfolded yesterday, I can't help but think that maybe some of this was meant to be."

"What do you mean?"

"I haven't seen my brother in a number of years. When we finally reconnect, it's to learn that he's the mate of the Prince. You come here in search of Zachary and find he's already been rescued, but had you known that you wouldn't have come here and met Beth."

"When you put it that way…" Gray said. "You might be right. It does sort of feel like this was destined or something. Can I ask you a question, though?"

Dawson shrugged. "Sure."

"Does it bother you?" Gray questioned. "Your brother taking a male mate?"

Dawson blew out a breath and seemed to be choosing his words carefully. "It doesn't bother me that his mate is male.

74

It bothers me that he kept that part to himself. That instead of allowing us to be a part of their lives, he purposely stayed away."

"Do you think you'll be able to forgive him?"

"I don't know. The three of us were always close. It hurt when he left. You know most felines stay solitary, but his leaving… It felt like he put his animal nature before his family. And now he has a whole new life that we're not a part of."

"Beth said something similar the other night."

Dawson smiled. "Beth and I have always felt the same. Family is the most important thing. We're humans first. Our parents were never there for us. Even when they were here, they always wanted to be somewhere else. I don't know if it molded our outlook, but I know I will never leave my son."

"Julian is a great kid," Gray assured him.

"Yeah. When I met his mom I thought we both wanted the same thing. And I think she did in the beginning, but it turned out she just couldn't stay. I still can't forgive her for leaving him."

Gray took in everything that had been said. He was finding out more and more about what Beth had been through, but he wanted, no, *needed*, the time to learn the things that only she could tell him. He wasn't sure that he was even going to get a chance. "Have you ever heard of two different species mating?" he asked.

Dawson tilted his head in thought. "I know a few who have mated with humans. Claude and Dorothy, as matter of fact. Plus Casey is a bobcat and Prince Zachary is a lion, but as for a wolf and a bobcat, I just don't know."

That was what Gray had figured.

"I guess you'll have to decide how far you want to take it," Dawson suggested, just as the ranger station came into view.

They repeated the same steps as yesterday, peering into the closed station before walking around to the trail that was barely there. Gray didn't get any sense of being followed, not even by Joe and Claude. So either the other two shifters were still pretty far behind or they were better at hiding their scent than he'd thought.

Gray and Dawson knew where they were going this time but still took the time to cover their tracks and double back to make sure they didn't lead anyone to the Prince's hideout.

They stayed in human form, so the trip up the canyon took longer than it had the day before. Several times they had to help each other up embankments where their animals had easily jumped. During the trek they took two breaks to drink water and eat a granola bar before they finally made it to where they'd run into the wolves and Casey. Just as he'd suspected, as they reached the area, RJ Cross was waiting there for them.

RJ jumped down, landing gracefully on his feet. "There you are."

Gray leaned against a rock and glared at him. Gray was in good shape, but the late night and second day of hiking up the steep canyon were taking their toll on him. His back muscles protested and his legs were starting to cramp. Meanwhile, RJ seemed full of energy.

"Where's the sheriff? Casey said he was coming with you." RJ practically bounced as he spoke.

Gray motioned behind them. "He's heading up with Claude. We split up so we could keep an eye out for if anyone was following."

"Cool!" RJ hopped back up on the ledge. "We need to get started before I die of boredom. Here comes Mike."

The other wolf stalked down in his animal form. He moved quietly, glancing behind him a few times. He shifted and seconds later a naked man stood in front of them all.

"I think they're here," he announced, accepting the bottle of water RJ handed him.

"About damn time," RJ muttered. "Time we finished this."

Gray exchanged looks with Dawson, not sure how he felt

about the upcoming conflict.

"They came through this morning as soon as the gates opened. They didn't take a map or ask about any of the trails. The ranger had the feeling they knew where they were headed."

"Are you sure it's them?" Gray had to ask.

Mike scowled at him. "Yeah, I sniffed around their vehicle. They're shifters and I recognized their scent from the cabin where we rescued Zach."

"So it's on." RJ clapped his hands together. "We need to tell Casey."

The other men nodded and they followed them to the cave they'd been to before. Joe and Claude would just have to catch up.

Casey greeted his brother with a hug and Gray with a handshake. Prince Zachary appeared tired but offered them a small smile as they entered the cave. The other feline stood at the far cave wall, rifle on his shoulder. Mike explained to the rest of them what he had seen and found out.

"So it's time," Prince Zachary acknowledged, although he seemed more resigned than RJ and Mike had been.

Casey rubbed his arm. "We capture these guys, then at least we know when we go back to get your cousin, there will be fewer complications. It has to be done."

"I just don't want anyone else hurt on my account," he told his mate, shaking his head sadly.

Casey wrapped an arm around his shoulders and pulled him off to the side of the cave. Gray hadn't thought about how all this affected the Prince. His own family had turned on him. Not only did he have to worry about every feline in the country but he had surrounded himself with traitors.

It was lucky for the Prince that he had such a strong mate in Casey. Almost a perfect match between them. It reminded him a lot of Kiley and Austin's relationship. Kiley had been a rogue shifter but had lived inside Gray's Pack territory. She'd only been close to him, Tyler and Tyler's daughter. But when she'd gotten together with an Alpha, all Kiley's experience in being rogue had allowed her to help understand some of the shifters Austin had adopted.

Austin and Kiley were a team, in much the same way as he witnessed Zachary and Casey acting. Gray craved that for himself. He shook the thought away quickly. First they needed to help the felines.

"How long to do you think it will take them to get up here?" he asked Mike and RJ.

"I figure about two or three hours, tops. It's one thing to map out the canyon and know where to go, but a whole other thing to do it when you're on foot. I knew where all the shortcuts were, and luckily they didn't or they would have beaten me here. I expect they'll come shifted. There are a couple of wolves, two cats and something else," Mike informed them.

"Something else?" RJ questioned his buddy.

Mike shook his head. "Couldn't get a good read."

"Joe and Claude should be here by then also. So five of them and nine of us — pretty damn good odds," Dawson stated.

"Seven of us," RJ corrected. "Craig stays with Zach to guard him. No one will get their hands on him again."

"I can take care of myself," Prince Zachary interrupted, coming back over. "You need Craig with you."

"Not gonna happen," Casey voiced, narrowing his eyes at his mate. "Above and beyond all else, you are the Prince of our people. Craig will guard you."

"I am also one of the most powerful cats in the world," Zachary argued back.

"No," Casey snapped. "You stay here."

"I'm sorry to get in the middle, Prince Zachary, but I have to agree with Casey. We need to finish this, capture these men and get you to safety. I have a son and sister who are dying to meet you. And you don't want to disappoint those two," Dawson added respectfully.

The Prince opened his mouth and closed it again. Finally, he nodded. "Nicely played," he grumbled. "You take after your brother more than you think."

Casey beamed and Gray hid his own smile. He could see the family dynamic coming together. It made him feel warm inside that Beth would have these men in her life.

"We should split up and take our positions. It might be a few hours, but we can't take any chances," Casey suggested.

The others all agreed. "Gray and RJ will take point. They'll take the farthest position," Casey directed. "Dawson and Mike will go south — block anyone from sneaking up on us that way. I'll wait for the sheriff and Claude. They'll cover the high ground."

"What about you?" Dawson enquired with a lift of his brow.

Casey grinned. "I'm bait. I'll lead them to us."

Zachary and Dawson started to protest, but Casey held up a hand to cut them off. "My show, my call."

"Sounds good to me." RJ grabbed a pack and threw it over to Gray. He caught it easily and glanced down at it. "Water and some beef jerky," RJ clarified. "Should hold us over till we see some action."

Gray shook his head at him but hefted the pack to his shoulder.

"I can't tell you how much I am looking forward to a hot shower and a nice home-cooked meal," his partner told him as he motioned toward the mouth of the cave. Gray didn't blame the man. Hadn't he just had the same thoughts? But at least he'd been able to rest in hotel rooms. He had the feeling that, during the search, Casey had kept his team off the radar and in hiding. Had probably had them sleeping on the ground the whole time.

Gray caught Dawson's eye and gave a slight nod. This was it. Hopefully everyone involved would be caught this time. Gray and the others would be able to get on with their lives. Gray clasped Dawson's shoulder and followed the young wolf out. He hoped everything went according to plan.

"Be careful," Gray murmured to Dawson. "Don't forget

your little boy expects you home tonight."

"My sister is counting on both of our returns," Dawson replied. "We'll be back and eating some of the best food in the world in a few hours."

Gray wished he shared Dawson's confidence.

Instead, as he followed behind RJ's bulk, he kept on high alert. This entire adventure had been very convenient and he didn't trust that everything would keep going smoothly.

Life didn't normally work that way. In Gray's experience, something always went wrong before it got straightened back out.

Chapter Five

While the canyon was truly a beautiful environment, the waiting was driving him crazy. It'd been two and a half hours since he and RJ had left the cave and still there was no sign of anyone else. There wasn't anything to do except keep a watch out and talk to the other wolf shifter.

"So you're retiring after this?" Gray asked the other man.

"Yeah, my older brother accepted an Alpha position in a Pack in New Mexico. Our Pack has so many strong dominants — and our Alpha has several sons who will take over the Pack — that my brother's name was mentioned as a replacement for the New Mexico Pack."

"You'll move with him then?"

"Yes." RJ crouched, flexing his fingers. "Dylan and our younger brother, Ben, are already heading there. After I've made certain that my team and the Prince are safe, I'll meet up with them."

"What are you planning on doing?"

"Ben's set up a storefront in town for me. I'll have the first tattoo shop there."

"Cool." Gray noted. RJ had enough ink to show that he enjoyed it. "Did you do all of the unit's tattoos?"

"Yeah, but my favorites are the two custom pieces I did for Zach and Casey. I'd like to do that more. Give mates something to show off."

Gray could imagine having a picture of Beth's sexy little bobcat on his body. Then he immediately saddened. It wasn't going to happen for him. A wolf and a bobcat? Gray was kidding himself. He'd get a couple of days with Beth, maybe even be able to stretch their time together to months. Eventually something was going to come between them. One of them would have to make the hard decision to separate. Gray needed to figure out if it was going to be worth it in the end to have Beth and have to let her go.

"I saw Zachary and Casey's tats. They're awesome," Gray admitted.

RJ chuckled. "Glad you think so. I'll give you a good price when you mate."

Gray bowed his head in thanks. "Appreciate it."

Of all the times for Gray to have connected with someone, any other point in his life would have been better. With the future of all shifters and their secrets being revealed, Gray couldn't abandon his Alpha.

"Sounds like some heavy thoughts over there," RJ commented.

"Yeah," Gray admitted. "Some things don't work out the way we want them to, do they?"

"I guess that depends."

"What do you mean by that?"

RJ shrugged. "The way I see it, we either chose the path we want to take and we fight like hell or we allow others to decide for us."

That was actually pretty wise.

"*Alpha red to alpha black,*" squeaked from the radio.

"Alpha black," RJ answered.

"*Headed your way.*"

RJ and Gray both stood and started to strip. In just moments, they had shifted into two big wolves, crouched and waiting. There was movement below them then a bobcat broke through the brush, hightailing it over fallen rocks. A squeal from ahead showed a large flying bird. RJ growled and jumped from his hiding place. Gray followed, barely landing before having to duck to avoid the large swoop the bird made.

He managed to stay on his feet right before a hard knock into his side had him sliding over the canyon ground. *Fuck, that's going to leave a mark.*

"Alpha red, alpha black," the radio went off again. *"Three more coming in from the south."*

Gray wasn't sure who that was, but he didn't have time to find out as he picked himself off the ground and faced the wolf that had run into him. He snarled at the animal. Bigger than him, the wolf was from the gray breed, but Gray would fight to the death if need be. He caught the wolf as he launched himself at Gray again. He got a piece of his leg and bit down, getting a huge paw to his head.

They scrambled around, each trying to gain the upper hand over the other. He could hear the sound of fighting around him. He wasn't sure who was there or even how many there were. He kept his eye on his attacker even when he made out the loud roar of a cat. He ignored everything around him and lunged.

Gray caught the wolf in the side, but his opponent managed to kick and get away. Gray stalked him before going after him again. He was pushing him toward the edge of the cliff. Gray didn't know how far it dropped, but it was his only option right then.

One last jump and he managed to roll the other wolf over. He heard the hit and peered over. The twenty-five-foot drop wouldn't kill him, but he would be out of the fight for a little while. Gray spun to go back to the battle, but a large feline landed on his back. He dropped, rolled and fought to get back to his feet, knowing he had a pretty good gash on his shoulder. An angry cougar crouched across from him.

Gray was used to being smaller than other wolf breeds, but this cat was huge. In all the years he'd been fighting Gray didn't think he'd gone one on one with such a powerful foe. It was going to take some quick moves and smart thinking to win this battle.

He growled and faked an attack. The cougar moved left, just how Gray wanted. He went in low, taking the cat's back legs out. He fell but swiped at Gray's side.

Caught by just the edge of the claws, he hissed in pain. Still, Gray wasn't giving up. In a series of quick moves, he went after the cougar again and again, backing him up the same way he had done with the wolf. The cat was smarter, though, and swung around to avoid going over the cliff.

A growl behind him, then a big black wolf rolled into the legs of the cat. Gray took the advantage and landed on the cougar's chest, taking him down. He closed his jaws around the cat's jugular and bit hard.

He was clawed at, but the black wolf butted the cat until the cat finally relented. Gray shook his head in warning before he let go. It was only then that he realized the sounds of fighting had ended.

Next to him the wolf — RJ — shifted to human form and straightened. "Damn, man — who thought a little wolf like you could fight like that?"

Gray glared at the other man but didn't really mean it. He was just thankful for the help. RJ grabbed the cat around the neck. "Shift," he ordered.

Gray took in the wreckage around him, noting four men on the ground with Casey standing over them. RJ hauled the cougar, now in human form, up.

"There's one more down there," Gray told him.

RJ laughed. "I don't think he's going anywhere for a while, but I'll get him."

He shoved the feline shifter at Gray. Gray escorted his prisoner toward the others as Casey was already on the radio.

"Good job, alpha blue. We'll come to you."

"Everyone okay?" Gray asked.

"There were more than we thought and they split up. These six, then another six who ran into Joe, Claude, Mike and Dawson. No one got to Zach," Casey told him.

"Anyone hurt?"

"Minor injuries." Casey gestured to him. "What about you?"

Gray's shoulder was screaming at him, but he'd heal. He also needed a fucking shower and some rest but he was alive. "Yeah, fine."

Casey cut his eyes to where RJ was hauling the wolf over his shoulder. "Let's move."

The trek down the canyon took a while with their prisoners' hands tied, but they made it. RJ would push at them occasionally but it was more for dominance than to hurt anyone further. Gray didn't really care what Casey or his team did to the shifters. It was over for him. Twelve men had been captured. The only one who should still be free was the Prince's cousin Raphael. Gray was pretty sure that Casey's unit could take the remaining man down without his help.

That meant his mission was finally over.

Gray could go home if he wanted to.

He didn't want to.

Now what the fuck am I supposed to do?

They reached the others and Gray didn't have any more to think about the future. The sheriff had his gun out, holding it on his own tied-up prisoners.

"Steve," Casey grunted at one of the men Mike was covering.

Steve scowled at him but didn't say anything.

"I see your dad didn't make the trip with you," Casey noted, crouching in front of him. "Too much of a coward to get his own hands dirty that he has to send his failure of a son?"

The man lunged at Casey, but Mike caught his shoulder and threw him back down.

"That's what I thought," Casey said in disgust, standing again. "You couldn't keep Zachary and now you've managed screw up the recapture. Your father is going to be pissed at you."

"Where is your father?" Prince Zachary joined them as he stepped down from the ledge above with Craig right behind him.

Steve, glared but didn't say anything.

"No worries. We'll get him," Zachary told Steve, grabbing hold of his chin. "While you and your friends here will be processed for kidnapping, torture and treason, I'll deal with your father."

Gray watched the scene closely. It seemed like he was the Prince's nephew. The family resemblance was close enough. More betrayal by family. Casey looked ready to kill Steve, but the Prince remained calm and cool.

"The rangers are on their way," Joe told them, pocketing his phone.

Gray collapsed against a rock. He needed to shift again to speed up his healing but wanted to wait until the prisoners were gone.

"You okay?" Dawson asked, coming up beside him with a noticeable limp.

"Good, you?"

"Fine." Dawson waved his hand. "Little shit had sharp teeth."

Gray chuckled.

"Who's got the beer?" RJ asked, falling in on the other side of him.

"First round's on me," Gray told him with a nudge. The other wolf had been a good man to have by his side. The training that RJ had been through had really saved their asses.

"I got the second," Dawson said, tiredly, from Gray's right.

"Damn, sounds good," RJ muttered, letting his head fall back and closing his eyes. "Sounds fucking fantastic. Do we really have to walk all the way back to the vehicles?"

"Pretty sure," Mike said joining them. "They aren't bringing in the choppers for us."

"But I'm tired," RJ whined.

"Shower, food, bed," Gray reminded him.

"Oh yeah. Race you?" RJ ran off cackling with Mike right behind him.

"Those guys are completely nuts," Gray commented.

Dawson snorted. "Yep."

* * * *

Beth knew the men were back. It was early evening and the talk of the town was all about the twelve men the rangers had taken to the jail for the sheriff. Dawson had gone home to shower while Gray had headed up the stairs ten minutes before.

"Why don't you go see if the wolf needs a little help?" Dorothy told her, passing over a room key. "I'll keep an eye on Julian."

She'd been sitting on one of the chairs in the great room, watching Julian color while kneeling over the coffee table. She accepted the key with a smile. Julian's attention was still on his artwork so she quietly left the room and headed up the stairs.

She hadn't noticed any lingering injuries on either man, but shifters healed fast. The rumpled and exhausted state the men had returned in testified to the tough fight they'd been through. Their quiet demeanor told of a hard day. Even when Gray had spoken softly to her, assuring her that he was unharmed, there had been a weariness in his gaze she'd never seen before from him. Beth quickly rushed up the stairs to the second floor and reached his door.

Gray's room was empty when she entered. She could hear the shower running in the attached bathroom. She left the key on the dresser and padded across the floor. The bathroom door was silent as she pushed it open. Steam billowed, but she could still make out Gray's naked body through the glass.

Shit, he has a fine body. She stripped and quietly opened the stall door.

"Damn, baby," he murmured. "I was just wishing you were in here with me."

She pressed against his back. There were several large scratches that had started to heal. It hurt her heart to see him injured. She carefully kissed the wounds. "I didn't get to wash your back last time. I thought I would volunteer my services again," she told him, sliding her hand over his stomach.

He chuckled and grasped the hand she was moving lower. "It's not my back that needs attention."

She smiled against his shoulder and stroked his hard cock. Gray moaned, thrusting his hips forward. He felt good in her hand. She liked that just the thought of her had him raring and ready to go. Beth glided around to his front to face him, keeping a hold of his shaft.

"It was just a day, but I missed you," he confessed quietly. Gray cupped her face and bent to run his lips over hers.

She rose to her toes. "I worried about you."

He kissed her sweetly, holding her close. Beth opened for him, let their tongues twirl and tease. As expected, the kiss quickly grew passionate and she gasped into his mouth as he ran his hands down her back to cup her ass.

She rocked up, letting go of his shaft and hanging on to his shoulder.

"Hold tight," he ordered, picking her up and pressing her back against the wet shower stall. He nibbled down her neck to her collarbone as she arched for him.

His hard cock poked at her entrance. She wiggled, letting him know that she wanted him inside her. Gray slipped in slowly, helping her open her legs around his waist so he could thrust deeply into her. Hot and solid, deep inside her. Beth gripped his shoulders hard, accepting him as he continued to gently enter her.

"You feel so good," he whispered against her flesh.

"So do you."

They'd made love before, but this time something felt different. It wasn't just the way he desperately plunged into her but the tears that sprang to his eyes.

"It's just us," she told him. "You and me. It's going to be okay."

Gray grunted before closing his eyes. "For how long?" His voice sounded wrecked. "How long before I have to leave?"

"It doesn't matter," Beth assured him. "We're together now!" She hoped he planned on coming back, but she knew that soon she would have to let him go. She tightened her grip even more. "All that matters is this moment."

"Beth…" He moaned her name as though he was in pain. Gray moved again, to pound deep inside, filling her like no one else, taking her to the edge.

"My Beth!" he called out, plunging his hips faster and harder.

"Gray!" She screamed his name as she climaxed.

"Not done," he told her, smacking off the water. Gray hefted her higher in his arms before elbowing the stall door open. They only made it as far as the bathroom rug before he laid her back and, still hard inside her, started to thrust once again.

"I can take it," she panted. "Give all of you to me. This once, don't hold back."

He growled and slammed into her once, twice, then one last time before releasing himself again. He collapsed on top of her, his panting matching hers and filling the small room.

"Don't let me go," he breathed out.

"No, no, I won't," she promised, hugging him close.

Beth didn't know how long they lay on the floor, but finally she started to shiver and Gray lifted his head.

"That was intense," he said, looking a little sheepish.

She giggled. "That was awesome."

He dipped his head and kissed her gently. "You are amazing."

She hummed, kissing him back. As long as he thought so, she was happy. Once they had broken their lip lock, he stood, lifting her with him and toweling her off before drying himself. Beth loved the attention he paid to her, making her feel so cared for. He was a strong man who showed gentle kindness.

Once dressed, they sat on the bed together while he held her hand, both not sure what to say.

"Beth…" he started but paused, pressing his lips together.

"It's okay, Gray," she assured him.

"I have to call my Alpha. Give him an update on what happened and have him pull the other wolves from the search. They need to know so they can go back to their families."

"I know."

He squeezed her hand. "When I call him, I want to tell him I'm not coming back right away."

"Really?" Beth was afraid of what that might mean.

"I think he'll let me," Gray told her. "I have been working my ass off for them."

"He'll also want you home. To go back to your Pack."

"I know," Gray said.

"Do whatever you have to," she said quietly.

The shrill sound of a cell phone interrupted their moment.

"That's Tyler," he told her, letting go.

"Do you want me to leave?"

"No." Gray gripped her hand. "I want you to stay."

She nodded and moved onto his lap and he reached for the phone on the nightstand. It was hard allowing him to speak to the one man who could send him away from her. She wanted to throw his cell across the room and hide him forever in her small town. But it wasn't her choice and she couldn't make him remain with her. Just like she needed her brother and nephew, Gray relied on his Pack and they relied on him.

He held her tight as he answered. "Hey, Tyler."

"Gray, are you okay?" his Alpha asked.

Beth rested her head against his chest, hearing both sides of the conversation easily.

"I'm good. You can let the others know that it's over for us. We captured twelve men. Casey Williams said they would be leaving soon to gather up the other men who were involved."

"Good, good," Tyler said over the line. "I called the sheriff's office and spoke to Joe already. I thought you would be there, but he said you headed back to your room to clean up. You weren't hurt, were you?"

Gray grimaced so Beth stroked his chest. "No, no—I've already healed. I just wanted to shower before I called you."

"Grayson." Tyler's voice took on a stern tone. "What is going on?"

Gray sighed and gripped her hand hard. "There's something I need to talk to you about."

"Okay," Tyler encouraged. "You know, whatever it is, I'll support you."

Gray blew out a breath but didn't continue.

Tyler waited a few minutes then a heavy sigh came over the line. "Just tell me."

"I want to stay longer," Gray admitted.

"I see. Tell me about her."

Gray laughed. "She's amazing and I'd like the time to get to know her better."

"Of course," Tyler said. "Take all the time you need. I think you deserve it."

"But what about the threats to the Pack?"

"Things have settled down lately. We're still on alert, but we're prepared to deal with anything that comes up. You deserve this time for yourself. Do you hear me? Don't worry about us."

Beth relaxed. She liked Gray's Alpha already.

"Yes, Alpha," Gray answered. "I hear you."

"Just make sure to check in with me. I want to know you're all right."

"I promise." He hung up the phone smiling.

"That was easy," she commented.

Gray let out a long breath. "I get the feeling he already knew. He didn't sound surprised at all. Maybe Joe said something?"

"I don't see why he would."

Gray frowned, but she wasn't going to let him dwell on what his Alpha did or did not know. She ran her finger over his furrowed brow. "Now, what should we do for the rest of the night?"

Gray's stomach growled and he blushed.

"I guess that's my cue to feed you," she teased, standing and offering her hand. "I think I can handle that. You'll need your energy for later, anyway."

"I really am hungry," he admitted.

Beth tugged him toward the door. "I think Casey and the other guys were coming for dinner too."

"It wouldn't surprise me. I get the feeling that those guys haven't had a good meal in a long time."

"Well, they're in the right place. Now, let's go before they eat everything in the inn," she told him.

Gray grumbled about needing a little bit more loving but followed Beth easily out of his room and down to the dining room. She held his hand and noticed for the first time how drawn he looked. He was starving. There was no telling how many times he'd shifted that day. Plus he still needed to heal.

She continued to drag him down the steps, the scent of food growing stronger until they reached the threshold to the dining room. Inside RJ, Mike and Craig sat at a large table already filled with overflowing plates.

RJ waved them over. "Dude, they have homemade chicken pot pie, mashed potatoes and rolls from scratch."

"I can see that," Gray said. "Did you leave any for the rest of us?"

"Maybe if you hurry," RJ replied. "Because I'm not going to stop eating until they roll me out of here."

Gray took the seat next to him, pulling Beth down beside him. She liked that he still hadn't released her hand yet. He wasn't ashamed of her. Instead, he was sort of staking a claim to her.

A part of her wanted that claim to be permanent. It might be too soon to even think about forming any kind of long-term bond, but in her heart she wished for it.

Dorothy and Julian walked in, hand in hand. Julian squealed, waving at them.

"Hey, little man," Gray called to the boy.

"I drew you a picture!" Julian came rushing over.

Gray accepted the picture and Beth glanced over his shoulder and down at the drawing of three cats and a wolf.

"That's me, Daddy, Aunt Beth and you," Julian told him proudly.

Gray lifted the boy into his lap. "It's wonderful! I love it, Julian." He rotated it more for Beth to be able to get a really good look as well.

"Great job, Tiny," she told her nephew.

"Really?" Julian sounded so excited.

"Really."

"Into your seat, Julian, so everyone can eat," Dorothy ordered him while she held a large tray of plates of food.

"Okay." Julian scrambled around to sit next to Beth and Dorothy filled the empty space in front of them with plates.

Gray groaned, bending so that he could sniff his meal.

"Told you!" RJ said smugly, leaning over and snatching one of Gray's rolls.

"Hey!" he protested with a laugh. Beth grinned along with him. She didn't see Dawson, Casey or the Prince but even she was starving after smelling their dinner.

"Homemade, dude!" RJ taunted, waving the roll at Gray.

Dorothy smacked the back of his head. "You behave, RJ Cross, or I'll be giving your brother a call."

"Yes, ma'am," RJ said, dropping his head. Beth noticed he kept the roll tucked in close, though.

Dorothy shook her head and smiled. "I'll bring you all a beer. I think you deserve it."

"Yay!" RJ cheered, digging back into his food.

Everyone laughed and Gray picked up Beth's hand, placing a kiss in her palm before he started on his own plate.

Beth ate more slowly than the men, making sure Julian was taken care of. The conversation remained light and playful, which she was grateful for. The guys needed a break from everything they'd gone through. Tomorrow was soon enough to figure out where they'd all go from here.

At least, that was what she thought, until Dawson strolled in with Casey and Zachary behind him.

"Look!" Julian pointed to the Prince. "It's the fancy cat!"

Dawson groaned, walking to his son's side. Everyone else laughed.

"Fancy cat," RJ repeated. "I like it!"

"Don't even think about it." Casey pointed to RJ. "He's still my mate."

"Sure, Cas." RJ held his hands up. "Or should I call you, fancy cat's man."

Casey stepped toward RJ, but Zachary caught his mate's arm. "Don't forget, RJ," Zachary said. "We know where your skeletons are buried."

RJ stuck his bottom lip out. "You're so mean!"

"No, he's not!" Julian defended. "He's going to take me a castle. A real one. He told me so."

"Well." RJ shook his head. "I guess I can't argue with that." RJ nodded at him. "You win, kid."

"Good." Julian nodded once before turning to his dad. "Sit down, Daddy."

Dawson caught Beth's gaze as they smiled at each other.

"Yes, son," Dawson said. "It's time we all sat and had dinner together as a family."

There was some shuffling of chairs and plates as another table was added to theirs to fit everyone. The place to the left of the Prince was empty until the small guard, Craig, walked into the room quietly and joined them.

Beth hadn't spoken to the strange cat shifter, but her brother had explained earlier who he was.

Once everyone was present, Dorothy arrived with a tray full of beer bottles and a glass of chocolate milk. She must have guessed that even Julian was getting into the celebration.

There wasn't anyone else in the inn's dining room, which was probably a good thing since Casey's unit was pretty rambunctious. Everything said was PG-rated, since there was a little boy in the room, but the guys amused her.

It was one of the best evenings she could ever remember having.

Dorothy quietly began to clear the dishes, with RJ and Mike getting up to help her. She tried to shoo them away, but they'd insisted. Julian started to yawn as he grew sleepy and Dawson pulled him onto his lap, patting his back.

RJ and Mike came back with more beer, but Beth waved away the offer. She leaned over and rested her head against Gray's shoulder while he spoke quietly to Craig.

There wouldn't be a lot of nights like this. The Prince had obligations and Casey's unit was breaking up and going their separate ways, but at the moment she believed all was as it should be.

If she didn't have the worry that Gray would soon be leaving her, Beth would be the happiest that she'd ever been in her life.

All she could do was enjoy the time with him.

If she worried too much about the future, she'd miss out on the present.

Gray tilted his head, brushing his lips over her temple. "Are you about ready to head upstairs?"

Beth was more than. "Yes."

"We're going to call it a night, guys," Gray said as he stood. He captured Beth's hand and helped her rise, too.

"Meet at eight?" Dawson asked. "We can head to the sheriff's office after breakfast."

Gray nodded before leading Beth from the room. Julian had fallen asleep on Casey's shoulder, but the rest of the men made hardly any comments as she and Gray walked from the dining room. Which she was a little surprised at, but thankful no one was giving them a hard time. Even jokingly.

She was fully aware that Gray was uncomfortable with the relationship between a wolf and a feline shifter. If anything other than the distance separated them, Beth suspected it would be the fact she was a bobcat.

Beth should probably have been upset about that fact, but for some reason all she wanted was Gray. It didn't matter how she got the man. He was hers. She was going to have to figure out how to make a relationship last.

Leaving Coyote Bluff was her worst nightmare. She loved the small town and the community that had become her sanctuary. No one there expected her to abandon her family like other feline shifters. Here she fit.

Gray had an Alpha and a whole other life she didn't know anything about.

On the quiet walk up to his room, she squeezed his hand. "Will you tell me about your Pack?"

The smile she received was beautiful, the love that shone through obvious. "Yes." He unlocked his room before ushering her inside. "How about we talk in front of the big window? We can enjoy the settling down of things."

Beth nodded. That idea sounded romantic to her.

While Gray opened the curtains and arranged the chair, she grabbed a couple of bottles of water sitting on the desk. Dorothy must have put them in earlier when she'd cleaned the room.

"There's only one chair in here," Gray told her. "I guess you'll have to sit on my lap."

Like that was a hardship for her. "Well, damn it."

He laughed before dragging her over to sit on him. With his arm around her back, she settled in to listen to him talk.

"I live in Colorado but far enough from the mountains that it's not too cold," he said. "Tyler, my Alpha, took over the territory from another Alpha who abused his Pack. Riker is now with our Alpha Council, paying for those crimes, and that leaves our Pack trying to move on from a bad beginning."

"That sounds horrible," she whispered.

Gray nodded. "Riker's Pack was so mistreated that when Riker was finally taken away, they ran as soon as they could. Another Alpha in Colorado opened up his own home to the members who needed to be away from the territory and memories and still wanted to remain a secret after the shifters unite and become public."

"So your Pack is coming out?" she asked.

"We are," Gray said. "It's not the best solution for everyone and I know that, but it's a start in helping shifters thrive. Austin, the other Alpha in Colorado, is taking in any wolf shifter who wants to join. He recently mated with a very good friend of mine."

The softness that showed up in his tone surprised her. "Was this friend a woman?" Beth questioned. Oddly, she didn't feel jealousy. Instead, she was bothered by the sadness in his gaze.

"Yes," Gray admitted. "Kiley and I were never meant to be together and we both knew it. We spent time together and we did have sex, but the emotional bond was missing."

"But you still loved her," Beth stated with certainty.

"I do, but as a friend. I'll miss her, but she's met the man she was supposed to be with. Austin is the perfect match for her. I'm very happy for the two of them."

"I believe you," Beth said. "I can see it in your face."

"If Kiley and I had settled for each other instead of allowing ourselves to search for who we're meant to find, she wouldn't have Austin and I'd have missed out on meeting you."

"And yet we barely know each other," Beth pointed out.

"True," Gray said. "However, the connection I feel to you is stronger than anything I've ever experienced. It's something that I want to explore."

Beth cuddled in to him further. "Tell me more."

"I work for the local police department there as a detective, although in the last year family obligations have kept me from working full-time. Even though my superiors are human and don't know about shifters, they've been great about giving me the time off I need. Although I don't know how much longer they'll be willing to do so."

"So, a cop, huh?"

"Yes," Gray said with a smile. "I enjoy the investigation

part of the work. Especially being able to swoop in and help someone who needs it."

"You're a hero."

"I wouldn't go that far. I just want to make a difference in someone's life," Gray admitted.

Beth didn't say anything about there not being much opportunity in the small town of Coyote Bluff for Gray to make that difference. Yes, they had a sheriff's department, but her town didn't have a whole lot of trouble. "Do you live with your Alpha?" she asked.

"No, I have an apartment in town that's closer to the station. Tyler has full-time guards who watch out for him and his daughter so I'm allowed to come and go."

"He's not mated?"

"Tyler?" Gray shook his head. "No, Jesse's mom was Tyler's college sweetheart and human. As soon as he told her about his shifting after she had Jesse, that was the end of it. She left Tyler and Jesse behind and they haven't heard from her since."

"But there's a chance Jesse won't be able to shift with one human and one shifter parent," Beth pointed out.

"I guess it didn't matter. Although we've learned that the shifter gene is stronger than her human DNA, so the possibility of Jesse shifting when she's older is pretty high."

"I just can't imagine leaving my child behind for any reason," Beth shared. "It seems like the worst thing a parent can do."

"I agree. We might have shifting abilities, but we're humans too. I think that's going to be one of the biggest hurdles we're going to have to face from pure humans. That we're just like them, with hopes and dreams, but we can transform into animals as well."

She shuddered just thinking about it. "I don't ever want anyone to know what I can do."

Gray didn't say anything for several moments. Then he placed a gentle kiss on her forehead. "I'm going to talk to Joe tomorrow and make sure he's aware of everything.

Without any time of contact with the shifters in charge of the movement, I don't want your town to suffer."

"Do you think we need to worry?"

"No," he said quickly. "I just want him to be prepared."

It was nice that Gray cared, but now Beth regretted bringing up the subject. So much could go wrong if humans freaked out about the knowledge of shifters. "Let's talk about something else."

"Sure," he murmured. "I think we'll have to get Jesse and Julian together soon. They're going to be the best of friends and I can see them both keeping us on our toes."

Beth laughed softly. "That might not be a good thing."

"It will be," Gray told her. "At least for us. We'll get to torture Tyler and Dawson, so that's a plus."

Beth closed her eyes as Gray continued to talk about the little girl back home who Julian reminded him of. She loved to listen to Gray's deep, rumbling tone while he spoke. Inside, she warmed at the thought of getting their two families in one place. There was hope for her and Gray.

Chapter Six

Glass shattering had Gray lurching up out of bed and fumbling for his clothes.

"What's wrong?" Beth asked sleepily, flipping the lamp on the bedside table on.

"Something's going on downstairs," he told her. "Stay here and lock the door behind me." Gray only pulled on a pair of sweats before he was racing out of the room. If he needed to shift, he'd be able to quickly.

Before he took a step down the hall, he heard the click of a lock at his door. *Good, at least Beth's out of danger.*

His instincts were screaming at him to use caution, so once he reached the stairs, he crept down in the dark. There was a scraping noise coming from the dining room. Gray didn't know what time it was, but certainty there shouldn't be anyone moving around downstairs.

If he'd heard the disturbance, Claude probably had as well so he'd have to make sure he didn't sneak up on the bird shifter.

At the bottom of the steps, he paused, peering into the doorway of the dining area. Nothing moved, but he faintly caught at least three different scents and breathing patterns.

Intruders. Gray was certain.

Across the entry, he saw a quick glimpse of movement. Claude was right next to the front door. Once Gray spotted him, it was easier to make out his silhouette. Claude nodded before dipping it to the side.

Gray held up three fingers in case Claude hadn't picked up their unexpected guests.

Claude motioned for him to move. Gray stalked forward

silently until he was just past the threshold into the dining room.

Felines, three of them straight ahead.

He dropped into a crouch and growled, letting his powerful wolf come to the surface enough that his sound shook the walls.

"Fuck! It's one of the wolves!"

Gray launched himself up and across the room, but whoever had been there a moment ago was already leaping through the open window. He heard the front door slam and figured Claude was chasing after the intruders from the front. Another feline dove through the opening, quickly followed by the third. Gray couldn't let them get away.

He was only a few feet behind, but as soon as he cleared the window pane Gray was knocked in the head with something.

"Shit!" He hit the deck hard and rolled just in time to avoid a boot to the back. Using his momentum, Gray kept out of his assailant's reach until he dropped into the yard.

"Asshole," Gray spat. There was no one on the porch, though. He stood and looked around.

He could smell the felines, but the scent was all over the place. It was as if they'd just disappeared. A light shining on him had Gray twirling around with a snarl.

Claude stood by with a flashlight in his hand, dressed in only a pair of boxers. "Where'd they go?"

"No idea." Gray peered around the yard again. "One stuck around long enough to hit me, but I didn't see him slip away."

The beam of the flashlight moved and Claude hissed. "You're bleeding."

Gray already knew that. Blood dripped down the back of his neck. "I know."

"We need to call Dawson and see what happened inside," Claude said.

Gray grunted but walked over to the steps before stomping up them. He couldn't believe the fucking felines had gotten away from him. Years of training and detective work hadn't helped him this time. He was pissed at himself.

"Come on." Claude gripped his shoulder. "We'll have Dorothy look at your wound."

"I'm fine," Gray grumbled.

"I insist," Claude replied. He stopped outside the front door. "Thanks for coming down."

"Of course. I'm just sorry that I let him get away."

"You didn't," Claude argued. "They had this planned. As soon I reached the porch, someone knocked me off my feet."

"Are you okay?"

"Fine." Claude waved his hand. "I knew there were three inside and didn't expect anyone else to be on look-out. I won't make that mistake again."

"How many total, do you think?"

"At least five," Claude answered. "And I've never scented them before so they're not from here." He pushed open the front door before strolling toward the dining room.

"Damn it," Gray muttered. "We need to warn the Prince. Whoever was here has to be after him."

"I agree."

Gray flipped the switch, bathing the dining room in the soft yellow light. "Son of a bitch!"

Every table in the room had been scored with some sort of sharp weapon. One of the vases had fallen and glass littered the floor. That must have been what had woken him.

"We stopped them from doing more damage," Claude said.

"But why?"

"To let us know they're here?" Claude suggested.

"That gave us a warning, though," Gray said.

"Yeah," Claude said. "I'm still trying to figure that out."

"Call Dawson," Gray told the bird shifter. "I need to let Beth know everything is okay."

As Claude headed one way, Gray walked toward the stairs. His head was pounding and he knew it was going to be a rough night, but he had to check on his woman.

"Beth!" He knocked gently on the door. "It's me."

She yanked the door open and stood there with wide eyes. "What happened?"

"Some felines broke in," Gray explained. "Claude's calling your brother."

"I smell blood." Beth grabbed his shoulder before spinning him around. "Gray!"

He chuckled to try and take away some of her worry. "I'm okay, I promise. Do you want to stay up here or come down and—"

"Dorothy needs to look at you." Beth grasped his hand then tugged him in the direction he'd come from.

Gray almost stumbled. *Damn, she can move fast.* "Slow down, honey."

"I can't believe that you're walking around like that."

He didn't get to say anything else because Dorothy was standing at the bottom of the stairs with her blue robe wrapped around her.

"Dorothy," Beth said. "Gray's been hurt."

"Claude told me. Bring him into the dining room. That's where your brother is going to meet us."

Gray decided to just let the women fuss over him since the more he walked around, the sicker he felt. He knew he wasn't injured badly, but it would take some time to heal. Beth led him to one of the tables off to the side where Dorothy had already set up some supplies.

"Sit here," Beth said ushering him to a chair. "You're getting pale."

"Feeling a little sick, but it'll pass," he admitted.

Instead of sitting next to him Beth kneeled between his legs before taking his hands in hers. Gray smiled down at her. It felt nice that someone was so concerned about him. Not that his Pack mates wouldn't be, but at home he had to be the strong one who watched out for the others. In Coyote Bluff, he was learning that everyone pitched in and it wasn't about species. The community he'd found himself in was certainly unique.

"Gray! You okay?" Dawson hollered as he walked in.

Gray waved his hand. "There's people sleeping, man. Keep it down."

"Not anymore," RJ said as he and Mike strolled in. "What's all the excitement about?"

Gray had forgotten that the two wolves were also sleeping at the inn. "Break-in."

"What?" RJ glanced around and snarled. "Are you fucking kidding me? With us in residence?"

"Where's the Prince?" Mike's question immediately followed RJ's rant.

"Casey and Craig are guarding him and my son at my house," Dawson stated. "We thought this might be a ploy to get Zachary out in the open and we're not going to do that."

"Why didn't they hit your place?" RJ questioned. He walked over to Gray and gently ran his hand over his shoulder.

With Beth still holding him and the comfort he got from RJ's wolf presence, Gray was able to relax while Dorothy began to clean his wound.

"More security," Dawson replied. "The inn has to allow their guests to come and go. Even though they lock the doors at night, there isn't an alarm. I caught the strange scent of some felines so I think they circled around my place but couldn't find a way in."

"We don't lock the windows," Claude said. "If they hadn't broken the vase, I wouldn't have even heard them."

"Me neither," Gray said.

"It's pretty stupid letting us know that they're in town," Mike commented.

"Unless they're not worried about us," Dawson said. "Joe's already on his way here. RJ, Mike, why don't the two of you watch my place. Let's not give the felines a chance at Zachary."

"You got it," RJ agreed.

The two wolf shifters didn't hesitate to walk out and toward the front door even in their half-dressed state. Of course, if they decided to shift, which Gray would have done, it would be easier for them not to have to undress.

"Now what?" Beth asked. "Are they going to come back?"

"I don't think so," Dawson answered. "I suspect they only want Zachary."

"How are we going to keep him safe?" she questioned.

Dawson chuckled. "I don't think we can. It took Casey literally sitting on him to keep Zachary in the house. He's so upset that anyone was hurt because of him."

Gray grunted. "Not his fault."

"When he finds out Dorothy's beautiful furniture was damaged, I expect he'll be hard to keep away from here," Dawson finished.

"Then you don't tell him," Dorothy demanded. "All of this can be covered up or replaced." She waved her hand around the room. "You just keep that sweet man safe. I want him and Casey coming back here more often and reconnecting with your family."

Dawson nodded. "I want that, too. First we need to end this fucking bullshit with Zachary's family. His uncle has to be behind this. We have his son, after all."

"What about the jail?" Gray suddenly had another idea. "What if this was to draw us away from there?"

"I just spoke to Joe," Dawson said. "All's quiet there. A couple of the rangers who live in town are helping us out. We have plenty of back-up."

That didn't give them much of a chance to play offense then. Gray hated defense, but if that was what it took to keep everyone in Coyote Bluff, including the Prince, safe, he'd do it. He glanced down at Beth. "I think it would be a good idea for you and Dorothy to go back to your house."

"But—"

"I agree." Claude joined them, putting his arm around his wife. "This was a stupid move and I think they're pretty desperate to get Zachary back. They lost the team they sent in and now they're scrambling. They might even consider taking either of you or Julian if they can't get to Zachary."

"Julian?" Beth repeated.

Claude shrugged. "I wouldn't put it past them."

"I'm finished here," Dorothy kissed the back of Gray's head. "Just let me put some clothes on and I'll go next door."

Gray waited until Claude and Dorothy exited before squeezing Beth's hands. "Watch over Julian. We'll all be keeping an eye on you all, but I don't want anything to happen to the two of you."

Beth nodded before he even finished his sentence. Gray knew that the threat to her nephew would have all Beth's protective instincts kicking in. The same as his were doing. "As soon as Dorothy comes back, I'll head over there."

"Not alone," Dawson demanded. "Claude will take you both. I want to go around with Gray to see if we can get the feline scents better."

"Not alone," Beth agreed. "Are you going to shift?" she asked, turning to him.

"I think that would be best," Gray admitted.

Beth sighed. "I wanted to see you in your wolf form again, but not under these conditions."

"When did you see him shift?" Dawson asked.

Beth blushed, causing a surprised laugh from Gray. Gray stood up and nuzzled her neck before turning to Dawson. "None of your business."

Dawson was smirking. "I think the two of you have been hiding things from me."

"Of course," Beth said. "That must be it. Because you know everything that goes on in this town."

Dawson frowned. "I used to."

Beth walked over to her brother. "None of this is your fault. It's a situation we were put into."

"That was caused by my — our — brother."

"You can't think of it that way," Beth said. "We have to protect Casey and Zachary like you would anyone else."

"I know," Dawson said. He glanced over at Gray. "Bet

you didn't expect all of this when you arrived."

Gray shook his head. "No, but I do know a thing or two about protecting those I care about. That's what being part of a Pack is. Let me help you and we'll put an end to all of this."

"So you're not leaving right away?" Dawson asked.

Gray didn't even need to look at Beth. He'd already told her so he just needed to let the others know. "My Alpha is letting me take some personal time. I'm staying in Coyote Bluff for a little while."

"Good," Dawson said. "It seems we're going to need you."

Gray was just glad that Dawson didn't question how long 'a little while' was since he didn't have an answer. No matter what, he wouldn't leave Beth or anyone else in Coyote Bluff while they were still in danger." "I'm going to take Dorothy next door," Claude called from the threshold.

"Hold up!" Gray hollered. "Beth's going, too." He turned to his woman and tugged her close. "Make sure you keep yourself safe."

"I will," she promised.

Gray kissed her deeply before pulling back then pushing her toward the bird shifter. "Keep an eye out on the walk. RJ and Mike should be out there already, but we don't know who else is," he told Claude.

Claude nodded.

Once the three of them exited, Gray nodded at Dawson. "You ready?"

"Yeah, let's do this." Dawson led the way onto the porch. Gray glanced round, but nothing seemed out of the ordinary. Would the felines actually have left the area already or were they waiting to pounce?"

"You shift first," Gray told Dawson. "I've got your back."

Dawson began to undress and within a few minutes he'd transformed into the small bobcat that Gray was getting used to. Once Dawson took a stance to guard Gray, it was time for Gray to shift. He did so quickly, not liking to be vulnerable for even a few moments.

Once Gray stood on his four furry paws, he saw the world differently. The instinct to hunt was strong. While Gray would normally push back his animal nature, this time he allowed the impulse to take over.

Not waiting to see if Dawson followed, Gray raced to the window where the three felines had gotten out. He sniffed around, pulling in the different odors. The felines hadn't been taking very good care of themselves. It was too easy to pick up the tang of unwashed bodies mixed with the feline scent.

He growled once then took off, following the trail he barely caught.

There was a scramble of some sort behind him. It sounded as though he'd surprised Dawson, but the bobcat was running after him. Gray was surprised to find the path leading away from Dawson's house.

His long strides ate up the distance until he was at the edge of the neighborhood. From his short time in Coyote Bluff, Gray was aware that if he kept going he'd end up at the canyons.

The fucking cats were hiding out close to where Zachary had been. It would take time to hunt them down. Gray paced back and forth, trying to determine if he should go now.

By morning, the scent would be gone. If he didn't get a head start, Gray wasn't sure what would happen next.

He glanced over his shoulder, finding Dawson watching him. He had the feeling that the bobcat would follow whatever choice he made. But it wasn't smart to go in with just the two of them.

A screech above his head startled him.

Gray peered up, spotting the hawk circling him. *Claude!* Okay, that was three against five.

A howl, then another joined it, and Gray knew RJ and Mike were closing in on them. *Damn it, they're supposed to be guarding the Prince.*

Of course, with Casey, Craig, Zachary, Beth and Dorothy all in one place Dawson's house was probably the safest in the town at the moment.

He waited for RJ and Mike to join him and Dawson.

RJ circled Gray, sniffing the air. He must have caught the same scents as Gray. He nodded once before tilting to peer at him. RJ was asking him what the plan was. Gray didn't want to take the time and energy to shift so he motioned his head toward the canyon, asking RJ's opinion.

RJ's wish to go after the felines came out clearly with his huff and bared fangs. He wanted to end this just as badly as Gray.

That worked for Gray.

Gray glanced over to Dawson, who nodded. Mike was doing the same.

Guess we're all in agreement.

Beth closed Julian's bedroom door quietly behind her. The windows were locked and she'd found his old baby monitor that they'd retired more than a few years ago.

"He still asleep?"

She glanced up at Casey, who was leaning against the opposite wall. It was so weird to see her oldest brother in her house. It wasn't like the home that they'd grown up in. Their parents hadn't ever tried to make their childhood as safe and comfortable as Dawson had for Julian.

Julian was really lucky. She was realizing that more every day.

"Yeah," she replied. "Out like a light."

"You want a cup of coffee?" he offered.

She snorted. "Why are you acting so weird?" He sounded overly polite.

Casey shrugged. "I don't know what to say. I left you and Dawson just like mom and dad did. I look at your lives here and know I made a mistake."

"You were our brother. It wasn't your job to look out for us."

"Wasn't it?"

"No." Beth walked to him. "It wasn't your job."

"I should have protected you. The way Dawson did. I should have found a place like this to take the two of you. I've missed so much. That boy in there doesn't even know who I am."

"It's not too late," Beth reminded him. "You're here now."

"And I've put you all in danger."

"But you came to family when you needed help," Beth pointed out. "You knew we'd have your back. We can build from there."

"I don't know if Dawson feels the same way."

Beth laughed. "He'll come around. He loves you. Every year on your birthday he takes a few beers out to the porch and drinks them while watching the sun go down."

"That's how I let him have his first taste of alcohol," Casey said quietly.

"And he remembers that. We both know what you sacrificed for us. Dropping out of school and getting your GED so you could work. We wouldn't have eaten without your help."

"It doesn't seem like enough. He was only eighteen, you'd just turned sixteen," Casey told her.

"And you had taught us how to survive."

Casey sighed. It didn't appear that any of her words were getting through to him. Beth didn't know how to make him feel better. She'd been devastated when he'd joined the military and left, but she also understood. Casey hadn't been ready to be a parent and he'd stayed. With Dawson aging to adulthood, Casey had walked away.

It was obvious to her that he was more like their parents than he wanted to admit. He relied too much on the feline part of him to make decisions. Beth wouldn't judge him, though. It was in his nature.

"Come on," Beth said. "Let's go downstairs so I can interrogate your mate."

"Right," Casey snorted. "More like he'll badger you for

stories about when I was younger."

"Cool." Beth took a few steps back. "There was that one time I caught you with Melissa Coolridge in my tree house."

"Don't you dare!"

With a laugh Beth raced off, Casey at her heels. She knew he was letting her win, but when she slid into the kitchen where Zachary and Dorothy were sitting at the table, she must have seemed half-crazed.

"What's wrong?" Zachary leaped to his feet. "Is it Julian?"

"No," Beth assured him. "I was just going to—"

From behind, Casey covered her mouth with his hand. "Nothing. She wasn't going to do anything."

Beth tried to pry her brother's palm away, but he dug his free fingers into her side, making her squeal.

"Fuck!" Zachary said then laughed. "The two of you are acting like children."

"Well..." Casey drawled. "I can show you—"

"Stop!" Zachary demanded. "There are ladies in the room."

"Sorry," Casey told Dorothy. "But Beth isn't a lady. She's my sister. Don't believe a word she says. Especially if it's about finding me in any compromising positions."

With a raised eyebrow, Zachary beamed. "Really?"

"Lies!" Casey stressed. "All lies."

"Let your sister go, honey," Zachary said. "I won't believe a word she says."

Casey grunted, but he did release her.

"Now," Zachary said, wrapping his arm around her shoulder. "Tell me everything."

"I hate you both," Casey muttered.

"I could always tell him about that time in boot camp during our twenty-four-hour leave," Craig stated, strolling into the room.

"Fuck!" Casey yelled. "I can't win."

"Oh, hush, you," Dorothy soothed, going over to coax Casey into a chair. "Let me get you some coffee and pie. I gave Dawson an entire cherry pie yesterday and there's some left."

"You're my favorite," Casey said to Dorothy. "I don't like the others at all."

Beth stared at her brother in shock. Her first memories of him were of Casey stirring mac and cheese from a box into a big pot. Casey had had to stand on a chair to fix them something to eat because their parents had been gone for a few days. Dawson had always been the brother who played with her while Casey had taken on the grown-up responsibilities.

She was seeing him in a different light now, though, as Dorothy fussed over him and Craig continued to tease. This was what Casey had needed. The freedom to be a little silly and play around. Having to take care of her and Dawson hadn't allowed Casey to have a childhood himself.

"He's really missed you," Zachary whispered from his chair beside hers.

She nodded. "We missed him, too. But seeing him like this, it's even better."

"I'm glad you understand," Zachary said. "He's struggled for a long time trying to come to terms with leaving you. I know he's tried to keep tabs on you both and when Julian was born, he almost came to visit, but he got called on a mission."

"I don't blame him," she admitted. "I just hope now he'll want to be a part of our lives. I don't want to lose him again."

"You won't, if I have anything to say about it," Zachary promised. "My family is so different from you and Dawson. I want Casey to reconnect with you both almost as much as he wants to."

She nodded, pleased. It appeared that Casey had really lucked out in the mate department. She and Dawson hadn't fared so well, but there was time. Beth peered out of the window, wondering what Gray was doing. It wasn't his Pack he was trying to protect. All of the drama and threats were directed toward Beth's own family.

Even though she hated that he was involved, Beth was also relieved he hadn't left yet.

Trust wasn't something that she gave easily. The fact that she absolutely did trust Gray meant a lot. It was her people, her community, that were being affected by the events happening. She knew he was staying for her, but still Gray had put himself at risk tonight.

She smiled at Dorothy as the older woman filled a mug and brought it over to him.

"They'll be okay," Dorothy said quietly.

"I know." Beth tried to sound sure.

"So, a wolf shifter," Zachary said. "How'd that happen?"

Beth smiled at her brother's mate. "I'm not actually sure. He came to help find you. I didn't expect anyone as interesting as him."

"From everything I've heard, Gray is an honorable man," Zachary offered. "I think it would be a good match."

She shook her head. "He has a Pack he has to get home to. I've never thought about leaving Coyote Bluff. I'm not sure how it would work between us."

Zachary glanced across the table where Casey and Craig were playfully arguing. "You might be surprised by how easily things can work out when it's meant to be."

"Is that how it was between you and Casey?"

"Yes," Zachary told her. "He came to my house with Craig during one of their time-off leaves. Craig's family has guarded mine for years, so I've been friends with Craig since childhood. I took one look at Casey and was immediately attracted. Then he opened his mouth and within five minutes, I want to punch him."

"Sounds like my brother," Beth said with a laugh.

"I still don't know how he managed to be respectful and a smart-ass at the same time. He deferred to my position, but he also didn't treat me like I was fragile. I'm used to people, especially felines, going along with anything I say. If Casey doesn't agree with me, he never brings it up in front of someone outside the inner circle. But as soon as we're alone, he has no issues with telling me what he thinks."

"That's great. I still can't believe that my brother is mated to the Prince of felines though."

Zachary blushed. "I hope soon you'll see me as just Zac. Maybe one day consider me as a brother," he confessed.

Wow! It was crazy that the most powerful feline in the United States actually wanted to be a part of her family. "I'd be honored to call you brother."

"Thanks," Zachary said then yawned.

Casey looked over and frowned. "We need to get some rest. Tomorrow is going to be another big day."

"I'm fine," Zachary argued. "I'm not going to sleep with our guys still out there searching for whoever broke into the inn."

"You're still recovering from your ordeal," Casey stated. He stood and walked over to Zachary. "Please just come rest."

"I'll be keeping watch," Craig interjected. "I'll make sure everyone makes it in safely."

Zachary appeared to want to continue disagreeing but finally sighed and stood. "Craig, please wake me if there are any problems. I don't care what my mate says."

Craig nodded. "Of course."

"I could beat you both unconscious, then we wouldn't have this problem," Casey muttered.

"That would be spousal abuse," Beth offered. "I'm pretty sure that's frowned on, especially when you're the mate of the Prince."

"Of course no one is on my side!" Casey exclaimed.

"I agree that you both should get some rest," Beth replied. "At least while you can."

"Fine." Casey held his hand out to Zachary, who immediately went to her brother's side. "If something happens—"

"I'll come get you," Craig promised.

Beth watched them both go before turning to Dorothy. "Let me show you where you can lie down. As soon as

Claude comes in, I'll send him to you."

"I'd appreciate it," Dorothy responded.

Craig nodded to her before strolling into the living room, where she suspected he'd be keeping an eye out for the others. Hopefully they would be returning soon.

* * * *

Two hours after Gray had been woken up, he followed Dawson up the steps to his front door. They'd managed to track the felines through the canyons into the area where several cabins had been built for tourists. It had been too risky for any one of them to search closely with several humans out and about.

At least they knew where to start later that morning after they had support from the rangers.

Either the felines were setting them up for a trap or they'd not considered how easily they'd be tracked.

Gray wasn't certain which option he would prefer. He'd love to end this entire ordeal and have the people responsible for kidnapping the Prince in custody, but after months of searching he didn't see things ending easily.

Before they reached the front door, Craig stepped out of the shadows.

"Everyone okay?" Craig asked.

"Yes," Gray assured him. "We have a good idea of the path they took and we'll follow up once the sheriff and rangers are available. We don't want to leave anyone vulnerable here when we track them down."

"Zachary's going to want to go along," Craig stated.

Gray would have, too. "That's up to him."

"RJ and Mike?"

"They want to keep watch. Dawson and I offered to switch places with them, but they insisted they could handle it," Gray explained.

"Right," Craig said. "If you ask them, they'll tell you that they don't need sleep." He held up a backpack. "I'm going to take them a few supplies. They at least need some food and water."

"Everyone asleep inside?" Dawson questioned.

"Yes, all is quiet. Where's Claude? Dorothy was waiting for him."

"He ran by the sheriff's office to get with Joe. He'll be here in a few minutes," Dawson explained.

"Okay." Craig started down the steps. "Try not to wake up Zachary or Casey. They'll never get back to sleep."

"We'll be quiet," Gray promised. All he wanted to do was climb in beside Beth and close his eyes. His head no longer hurt, but he was more tired than he could remember being in a long time. Not only was he physically exhausted, which he could push through, but the worry and stress for Beth and her family were taking a toll on him.

"Come on." Dawson slapped his shoulder. "I'll show you to Beth's room on my way to check on Julian."

Gray nodded. That worked for him.

The house was homey and smelled of coffee and pie. He hadn't gotten to visit before so it was nice to see where Beth lived. After a few hours' sleep, he'd appreciate it even more.

Dawson didn't give him a tour. He just led the way until the two of them stood in front of a door. "Here's Beth. Julian is right next door and I'm across the hall. Try to sleep some and we'll regroup in the morning," he whispered.

"Will do," Gray agreed before turning the knob to enter Beth's room.

It was dark inside, but he stood by the entrance until his eyes adjusted. He could see her bundled under the covers lying on the right side of the bed. Gray stripped off his sweatpants then walked over and climbed in beside her.

When he lifted the blankets, Beth murmured softly.

Gray pulled her closer until her head was against his chest. He needed to feel the connection between them. So much could have gone wrong earlier. If he hadn't heard the broken glass, the felines might have attacked them inside the inn.

He would have done his best to protect her, but he didn't like the fact that she'd been anywhere near danger.

Anger began to build in him.

Fucking cats are going to pay for what they've done.

"Shh," Beth whispered, patting his chest. "Everyone is okay. Get some sleep."

"Sorry." He hadn't meant to wake her, but the tension didn't seem to be leaving his body.

"It's okay." She lifted her head, looking at him. "Did you find them?"

"Maybe. We at least have an idea where to start the search."

"Good. Now close your eyes. You won't be any help if you're worn out."

"Just let me hold you," he said. "That will help me relax."

Beth didn't respond with words. Instead, she wiggled around until her leg was over his and she was cuddling into his shoulder. She still smelled fresh and clean from their shower earlier and he breathed in her sweet aroma. That seemed to help his body calm, so he did it again.

For several minutes, they lay there holding each other. Finally she went lax and he knew she'd fallen back asleep.

He strained to hear anything else in the house, but all was silent.

RJ and Mike would make sure they were warned if the felines came back. Gray hoped that Claude and Dorothy remained over here instead of going to the inn by themselves. He should have spoken to the bird shifter about that before Claude had left to update the sheriff.

He finally felt sleep starting to tug at him and closed his eyes. Hopefully this time he wouldn't be woken up for several hours.

Chapter Seven

Gray woke up and stretched, still feeling tired but somewhat refreshed. Beth wasn't in bed with him, which was disappointing, but he could also smell bacon being cooked so that was something.

He sat up to peer around the room. Gray hadn't gotten a good view in the dark, but with the sun already risen behind the curtains, he grinned. Beth had every flat surface covered with some sort of knickknack.

The décor was simple, with black furniture, black curtains and several black and white photos, but the splashes of color were amazing. The sheets over the mattress were red, as was the rug in front of the door.

The cluttered and unorganized state of the small items scattered around spoke to him of how lived-in Beth's area was. He liked it. His own apartment was spartan and while Gray tried to find pieces to make it more homey, he'd never quite managed to get the right feel of the place. Beth might be able to help him. Or maybe he already found where he was meant to be.

Gray was going to have to do some serious thinking about his future. As much as he loved his Alpha and home, Gray couldn't deny that Coyote Bluff seemed to fill a hole in his life.

A loud, fast knock sounded on the door before it swung open.

"Wolf! Wolf!" Julian ran inside. "We have bacon!"

Gray laughed as he discreetly made sure his naked lap was covered. "I smelled that. I was hoping there was still some left for me."

"There is," Julian told him. "I wouldn't let RJ eat any yet. He tried to steal some from Aunt Beth."

"He did?" Gray mock-growled. "I'm going to have to get him."

Julian froze. "You're not going to hurt him, are you?"

Gray frowned. He'd thought they were joking around. "Hey, come here."

Slowly, Julian walked over to the side of the bed. Gray reached down and plopped the young boy down where Beth had been earlier. "You know that no one here is going to hurt you or anyone else, don't you?"

Julian shrugged. "We had this wolf come through one time and he picked a fight with everyone. Even Daddy and Claude. He wasn't a nice man."

"Well, I promise that I won't be mean to anyone in this house," Gray vowed.

"How come you didn't say that you wouldn't be mean to anyone ever?" Julian questioned. "Shouldn't you promise that?"

Jeez, this kid was smart. "Because I don't want to ever break a promise to you," Gray told him. "But if someone tried to hurt you or your aunt or someone who couldn't defend themselves, I might have to get mean. I wouldn't hurt them too bad, though. And I'd call the sheriff to come help."

"Like Dad?" Julian pressed. "You'll only be mean to bad guys?"

"Yes," Gray said. "Just to bad guys."

Julian grinned. "Okay. That's good."

Gray was glad that the tense moment had passed, but he really needed to get the whole story from either Beth or Dawson. Several times now Gray had gotten the feeling that the residents of Coyote Bluff had had previous trouble with his species. That might need to be brought up before the Council. The community there should be protected.

"How about you go make sure there's fresh coffee, and I'll be right there," Gray suggested.

"Okay!" Julian was off the bed, running down the hall in an instant.

"Hope no one else was sleeping," Gray murmured with amusement. There was just something about Julian that made him smile. He really did want to get Julian and Jesse together to see how the two kids got along. Throwing the covers back, Gray spotted his sweats laying across the end of the bed. Beth must have picked them up off the floor when she'd woken.

Gray pulled the soft fabric on before strolling out of the still open door. He'd need to shower and change in his own room before heading out to search for the felines responsible for the inn's damage, but first, coffee and bacon.

As he stepped into the hall, Dawson was coming out of his own room.

"Julian woke you up?" Dawson asked.

"Nah," Gray said. "I was actually already awake, but he did promise me bacon."

"Ah," Dawson chuckled. "The kid does love his bacon."

"As every growing boy should," Gray teased. He could hear RJ's laugh and Julian's squeal of delight. "But I have a feeling that if we don't hurry, RJ might charm some before we get ours."

"Come on." Dawson clasped his shoulder before shoving him forward.

It reminded Gray so much of the camaraderie of Pack that he had to keep from stumbling. How had he gotten so comfortable so quickly? This was just supposed to be a quick stop before finally being able to go home. Now everything was changing.

"I hear there's bacon!" Gray called as he entered the kitchen.

Beth whirled from the stove, spatula in hand as RJ was standing by the table holding Julian up over his head. Zachary sat at the table, nursing a mug. "That's the rumor," Beth told him.

Gray stalked forward, brushing against her to kiss her

quickly before he snagged a piece of bacon from the paper towel where it had been cooling.

"Hey!" She swatted at him, but he merely grinned back.

"No fair!" RJ exclaimed.

"That's cheating!" Julian cried.

Zachary was chuckling.

Gray just chewed the crispy bite, ignoring them all. Beth looked beautiful standing there glaring his way.

"Where's everyone else?" Dawson asked, passing by him to the coffeepot.

"Casey and Craig are outside keeping an eye on the house and inn, making sure the felines aren't around, and Mike's in the shower," Beth informed them.

"Claude's not here?" Gray asked.

"They went home last night," RJ said. "Mike kept an eye on the inn to make sure there wasn't any more trouble."

Gray nodded. He'd suspected Claude wouldn't want the inn to remain empty, but he hated that the bird shifter didn't have any back-up. Especially with a human mate to protect.

"They're coming over for breakfast," Beth said. "Dorothy was just finishing up some muffins."

"I hope she made chocolate chip!" Julian said. "They're my favorite."

RJ set the boy back down in a chair. "I don't think Gray should get any. He stole food."

"Yeah!" Julian agreed. "I should get his."

Gray laughed loudly. "Is that so, little man?" He tickled Julian's belly as he sat down beside the boy.

"No," Julian said. "You can have a muffin. I was just kidding."

"I know." Gray ruffled the kid's hair. "Next time, I'll steal a piece for you."

"Deal!" Julian said.

"No stealing necessary," Beth admonished them. "Here you go." She set a platter of meat on the table before going back to the counter and picking up two bowls. One held fluffy eggs and the other crispy fried potatoes.

Gray groaned. All this good eating was really going to have an effect on his waistline.

There was a knock then the front door opened.

"Good morning!" Dorothy called out.

"We're in the kitchen," Dawson hollered. "Come on."

"You have felines hunting the Prince and the door was unlocked?" Gray asked.

RJ snorted. "Craig wouldn't have let them close had they been a threat."

Gray shook his head. He hadn't gotten to see Craig in action, but the way Craig stalked about, he had to be some sort of badass. It made his curiosity peak.

"Just wait," RJ said as if he was reading Gray's mind. "Craig is trained in every sort of martial art there is. He was groomed to protect Zachary."

The Prince nodded. "He really is talented."

"Okay." Gray shrugged. He'd have to take their word for it.

"How's everyone doing?" Dorothy asked as she entered the kitchen. Claude was behind her, carrying a large plate. Gray could smell the fresh-baked goods already.

"We're fine," Gray answered. He glanced at Claude. "Everything okay at the inn?"

Claude smiled. "Yes. I already have some guys from town cleaning up and taking out the ruined furniture. We'll be closed today, but I plan to reopen tomorrow morning."

"I told him that I could just cover up the damage with a tablecloth, but Claude's been wanting to update the décor in there anyway. Now's as good a time as any," Dorothy said.

"Chester Grant makes some hand-carved wood tables that I think would go well in the dining room," Claude said. "He's got several in stock and can have them delivered today."

Dawson patted Claude's back. "It'll help him toward sending his girl to college as well." Dawson glanced at Gray.

"Chester's daughter was accepted into Yale. It's expensive, but she did get a partial scholarship."

So Claude didn't really need the new tables, but he was buying them to aid a community member. Gray nodded. "I'd like to see some of his stuff. I still need to get Austin and Kiley a mating gift."

"That's a great idea," Dorothy praised. "I'm sure Chester would know exactly what a new couple would need."

Beth squeezed his shoulder.

A sense of peace filled him.

Pack, community, family — it didn't matter what word was used. This closeness could only come from good people who truly cared about one another.

"Now everyone sit down and eat while it's hot," Beth ordered.

For several minutes there was laughing, teasing and the clang of utensils on dishes before everyone was seated.

"Chocolate chip!" Julian cried. "I knew it."

"Woo-hoo!" RJ called.

"There are also blueberry, orange cranberry and oatmeal," Dorothy said.

Julian made a face. "Yuck! I think you should only make chocolate chip."

"I don't know," Gray said taking an orange cranberry. "These look really good." They were his favorite, as a matter of fact.

"Nothing is better than chocolate chip," Julian informed him.

"I'm with the kid," RJ said. He reached over and picked up two of the muffins, dropping one onto Julian's plate before biting into his own. "Jeez," he muttered with a mouthful. "These are delicious."

"Okay, children," Dawson drawled. "Eat your breakfasts. We have to meet up with the sheriff in half an hour. Julian, eat some eggs, too. Don't fill up on muffins and bacon."

Gray chuckled before bending over his plate to finish his own meal. He still wanted to check on Claude and Dorothy before they headed out.

Beth wiped down the last countertop before tossing the sponge into the sink. Julian was still coloring peacefully at the kitchen table so she had a few minutes before he was dragging her across the yard over to the inn.

Neither Dorothy nor Claude acted as though the damage to the inn was a big deal, but Beth knew how much they loved the place. When no one else had accepted a hawk shifter and human mating, Claude and Dorothy had set out on their own to make a life together, without any support from either of their families.

Now it appeared that Casey had steered the couple toward Coyote Bluff, but Beth couldn't even be mad about that. Claude and Dorothy were happy and the residents of Coyote Bluff had gotten to adopt the loving pair. It was a win-win for everyone.

Dorothy and Beth were going to spend the day rearranging and redecorating the dining room of the inn. By the time it reopened, Beth hoped that Dorothy would be able to put last night's events behind her.

"Are you ready to go next door?" Beth asked her nephew.

"I am!" Julian said, jumping off his chair. "Claude said I could help him pick out new chairs to match the tables."

"Wow! That's a pretty big job."

"Yep." Julian nodded. "But I can do it."

"Yes, you can." Beth ruffled his hair. "Let's go, then."

Julian took off toward the front door.

"Stay close to me," Beth ordered. Usually they let Julian run between their house and the inn, but with the felines still out there, Beth wouldn't take any chances.

"I know the way!" Julian argued.

"Julian!"

He had the front door open before she'd crossed the threshold from the kitchen.

"Julian, stop!" she yelled. She raced after him, but he was already down the steps and in the yard. "Julian!"

He stopped and spun around. "What?" he whined.

"Come back here," she said sternly. It wasn't often that she had to discipline him but he was getting close.

Julian slumped his shoulders. "Sorry."

"Let me lock up," she told him. Beth set the alarm before checking to make sure she had the keys, then secured the door. After she was certain no one would be getting inside in her absence, she turned. Julian was still in the same spot with a frown on his face, but something felt off.

Beth glanced around, close to panic. The hairs on the back of her neck were standing up as the feeling of being watched hit. "Julian," she said quietly. "Hurry here."

Julian must have heard the tremor in her voice, because he immediately took a step forward.

A tall, raggedy-looking man leaped out from the side of the house.

"How about the boy comes to me instead?" he said.

"Aunt Beth?" Julian's frightened voice was high.

Two growls cut off his words.

Shit! Julian was several feet away and the animal sounds were coming between them. Beth walked forward until she could peer down the deck stairs. A large tiger and jaguar stalked from the other end of the yard. They were heading right toward her nephew.

"What do you want?" she demanded of the stranger.

"You and the boy will do for now. I'm sure the Prince will cooperate better for your safe return." He grinned, showing off yellow-stained teeth. "Of course safe could mean so many things, now, can't it?"

"Who are you?" she asked. If she kept his attention on her, maybe Julian would be able to run. Claude and Dorothy had to be close by.

Beth couldn't believe that they were in this situation to begin with. Dawson and Gray had warned her, but Beth hadn't actually thought anyone would come after her or Julian. The guys had left to track these felines down.

"My name is Dustin and you're going to listen to

everything I say or my friends there are going to tear that little boy apart."

Julian was starting to shake and tears filled his eyes. "I'm sorry, Aunt Beth."

"It's okay," she told her nephew. "You just be strong." She glared at Dustin. "Let him go and take me."

"Oh, how brave," he mocked. "But I don't think so. We'll have our fun with you and not harm the kid as long as you listen. You try and get away and we'll rip his throat out."

Her stomach roiled when Julian whimpered.

"It's okay, Julian," she called out. Beth was on the edge of the deck now. All she'd have to do was jump to place herself between Julian and the strangers. She was not going to let them take her nephew.

"No, it really isn't," Dustin corrected. "Leo! Watch the girl."

The tiger turned to Beth and snarled. Okay, she really didn't want to feel those teeth.

"Kip!" Dustin called. "Grab the boy."

The jaguar stepped toward Julian.

Oh, hell no! Beth growled and launched herself off the porch. She flew over both felines' heads and landed, blocking them in that way from Julian.

"That was stupid," Dustin said.

"You're not touching him," Beth said.

Dustin walked toward her. "You're just going to make things harder on yourself."

"When I say go, I want you to run as fast as you can toward the inn," Beth whispered to Julian. "Scream for Claude."

"Okay." Julian sounded so scared. She hated these fucking guys who were threatening them.

Beth knew she was no match for any of the powerful shifters. The tiger and jaguar could both take her smaller bobcat form down quickly. Dustin smelled like panther, which was just as bad. She had no chance of escaping without injury. But she was going to fight for her life.

"Come quietly and we'll leave the birdy and human

alone," Dustin taunted.

"Go!" Beth pushed Julian toward the inn while spinning to face Dustin. "You're not taking him."

Dustin laughed.

"Julian, duck!"

A gun shot rang out and Dustin and the two cats froze.

"Hurry, Beth!" Claude yelled.

Oh, thank God! Julian was almost to the porch where Claude was standing, still aiming the weapon at Dustin.

She took off at a sprint, but before she could get halfway across the yard the tiger leaped at her. Beth hit the ground with the massive animal on top of her. Claude fired the gun again, but Beth was in a fight for her life.

* * * *

They'd confirmed four people were inside the rented cabin and one of them was the man who'd been responsible for the entire ordeal Zachary had been through. Zachary's cousin was in the living room watching television while three of his men sat at the kitchen table playing cards.

Gray knew they were missing some of the other shifters, but they'd be easier to find once they got these men into custody.

The excitement from Casey and his team was catching. They were so close to ending it all.

Now, with the help of the rangers, they'd tracked down the last threat to the Prince.

Casey pulled out his weapon, a Desert Eagle, and met Gray's gaze. Gray nodded and waited while the other man held up a hand to the other members of the unit behind him. Five seconds. He watched Casey's fingers come down one at a time until he held up a fist. Once the countdown was up, they moved into action. Casey kicked in the front door and Gray heard the other part of the team break down the back door. They ran into the cabin, weapons drawn and ready.

There, in the center of the living room, was a man who appeared similar to Zachary. He appeared shocked to see them, but the surprise didn't last long. He leaped to his feet but Casey strode across the room, slapping him back down.

"Cas," Zachary said. "Let me handle this."

Casey glanced over his shoulder. Gray made sure to stay at Casey's back while RJ and Mike flanked the Prince. *Zachary should have the opportunity to face his cousin.*

"Raphael," Zachary said with a growl. "You're not looking too good."

"You've been better yourself," Raphael responded. "Lost some weight? You must not have been eating well lately."

Casey growled.

"It's okay, Cas," Zachary said, not turning to his mate. He was still stared at his cousin. "I doubt Steve is faring well in jail."

Raphael snarled. "You'll pay for taking my son."

Casey laughed. "He didn't even put up a fight. I always knew he was a coward, but he rolled over and ratted on you before we asked him one question."

"He'd never betray me!" Raphael spat.

"The night you took me from my suite, you deposited ten thousand dollars into an off-shore account. It's your back-up plan in case you failed. I even have the account number now. Steve's told us everything."

"No." Raphael paled. "He wouldn't."

"He did." Zachary crouched in front of Raphael. "It's over."

Suddenly, Raphael smiled. "Perhaps." He glanced toward Casey. "But it's too late for you to save everyone."

Casey straightened. "What's that supposed to mean?"

"You might have captured me, but at what cost, Prince mate?" Raphael said. "Even now my best three fighters have your sister and nephew. Do you know how easily a tiger's jaw can pierce a skull? You're about to."

Gray didn't hesitate. He ran for the front door. Dawson was already in front of him.

"The truck!" Dawson yelled. "It'll be faster."

Gray sped for the open driver's door and had the vehicle started and pointed back toward town even as Casey dove into the passenger side.

"Hurry!" Dawson cried.

"Claude is there. He'll protect them," Gray said. He was speaking the words for Dawson's benefit but even to his own ears they sounded hollow.

"I shouldn't have left them," Dawson said.

"It's going to be okay," he said. "They'll be fine." He couldn't pay attention to Dawson freaking out or he would lose his mind. He was telling himself the same thing. Surely with the rangers and Casey's entire team at the cabin in the canyons, someone could have stayed with Beth and Julian.

Gray hadn't truly believed that they'd be targeted. The actions from the night before had been stupid, leaving Gray to believe the felines were desperate and not thinking straight. Now things were different.

While they'd gone after Raphael, Beth and Julian had been by themselves, in real danger.

Of course Raphael could be full of shit and just fucking with them, but that didn't explain the shifters missing from the cabin.

Even if Beth and Julian were at the inn, only Claude would be there to fight against three powerful cats.

Gray took a turn too fast and the truck skidded along before the back end slid. Instead of slowing down, he pressed his foot harder on the accelerator. Nothing mattered other than getting to Beth and Julian.

"Take the next left." Dawson pointed ahead. "It'll take us to the front of the inn quicker."

"Okay." Gray yanked the wheel, taking the short cut. Fuck, it felt as if an hour had gone by instead of just a few minutes.

Dawson had grown quiet and Gray couldn't even imagine how he felt. Gray was scared shitless for the woman and kid, but this was the family that Dawson depended on.

Gray felt as though he'd failed them all.

The entire point of his staying was to spend more time with Beth and make sure that her family remained safe. Instead he'd majorly miscalculated.

"Almost there," Gray muttered. He pulled the truck onto the main road blocks away from the inn. "Damn it! Call the sheriff!" Why hadn't they thought of that before? Joe wouldn't have made it before them since he was at the station on the other side of town, but someone else might be close by.

Dawson was struggling to remove his phone from his pocket as Gray continued to speed down the road.

In the background he heard Dawson talking, but it took all his concentration to maneuver them safely without crashing. The driving training he'd received from the police department was coming in handy and he'd have to remember to thank his boss.

Up ahead, he could see the top windows of the inn.

Gray slammed his foot on the brakes and the truck fishtailed, coming to a stop almost landing in the yard.

His breath caught at the scene in front of him.

Dorothy's prone body was laid out on the deck of the inn with a large hawk sprawled out close by. He didn't see Julian, but Beth was in her bobcat form, facing off against a tiger.

Blood dripped from a long gash in her leg and she was limping, trying to avoid the claws of the bigger cat.

Gray kicked his door open and climbed out quickly. He ripped the clothes off his body while calling forward his wolf. His shift came faster than ever before. On all four legs, he howled deeply before charging toward Beth and the tiger.

Beth heard the squeal of tires, but she couldn't take her attention away from the tiger. Claude had managed to take out Dustin before the jaguar had attacked him. After that it had been pure chaos.

The only reason she was able to fight the exhaustion and pain was because she knew that if she didn't, this fucking tiger would be going after Julian next.

She'd lost track of her nephew but had to believe he was still safe.

The eerie wolf howl had her almost missing the swipe of the tiger's sharp claws. She managed to duck out of the way just in time. From the corner of her eye, she glimpsed the figure racing toward her.

Oh shit, I can't deal with another attacker.

Instead of coming at her, the wolf launched himself onto the tiger's back and she realized it was Gray. *Oh, thank God!*

She glanced in the direction Gray had come and saw Dawson scrambling toward her. The vicious sounds of the fight between Gray and the tiger echoed around the yard. Beth stepped forward, but her back leg buckled and she collapsed to the ground.

Dawson nudged her as he came to her side. She shook her head and hissed at him. He needed to find Julian and make sure that the boy was okay. Both the jaguar and Dustin, still in human form, were down, but she knew Dorothy and Claude had also been hurt.

"Stay still," he told her. "Where's Julian?"

She shook her head. The last she'd seen her nephew, Julian had been tumbling underneath one of the bushes.

"I'll find him," Dawson said. "Help is on the way."

Beth yowled, responding the only way she could. Dawson must have taken that as acknowledgment, because he stood up.

"Julian!" he yelled. "Where are you, son?"

"Daddy?"

Beth rotated her head and saw Julian climbing out from under a rose bush. He was a little scraped up but seemed okay.

"Julian!" Dawson's relief was evident in his voice.

Her nephew looked from his dad to her and burst into tears. "Daddy."

She wanted to go to the boy, but the pain was radiating from her leg to all over her body. Beth had never been hurt so badly. There was nothing life threatening, but she was going to be feeling this later.

A yelp took her attention back to Gray and the tiger.

Gray had done some damage to the large cat.

While Beth had mainly just been trying to keep the tiger's attention on her and move fast enough to avoid injury, Gray was aggressively lunging and catching the tiger with his sharp canine teeth. She was a little surprised that he could keep up with the large cat. Wolves were so powerful because they hunted in packs. It was obvious that Gray had been highly trained and that he was using those skills against the feline.

The tiger caught Gray in the leg but Gray managed to slip away. He needed help or he'd end up as exhausted as she was.

Beth tried to rise, but as soon as she got to her feet, her back leg went out from under her. She grunted as she connected with the ground.

Gray looked over to her and howled.

Two answering calls came loud and clear.

Beth tried to scramble away from the fighting but had only managed to drag herself a few feet when two more wolves ran into the yard. They immediately went to Gray's aid and the three wolves surrounded the tiger.

It had to be RJ and Mike. Gray's back-up had arrived.

In the distance, she could also hear sirens headed their way.

Finally, help was coming. She'd managed to hold off the felines and Julian was safe in his father's arms. From her spot on the grass, she could see Claude was awake and transforming back to human and Dorothy sat holding Julian's hand. The three wolves were keeping the tiger pinned to the yard, not letting him up.

The sheriff parked in the driveway, cutting off the siren before exiting his SUV. He held a Taser in one hand as he stalked toward the battling shifters.

"Back off!" Joe ordered.

The wolves were snarling and barking, but they did give the sheriff room. When the tiger lunged at Joe, he pulled the trigger of the Taser and two probes extended from the small device and attached to the cat's stomach. Electricity buzzed.

At long last, the tiger stopped attacking. Instead, he dropped down, panting hard and whimpering.

"That will hold him for a few minutes," Joe said. "It'll give me time to tranq him."

The two bigger wolves took on a guard position over the tiger, but the small one, who she knew was Gray, ran toward her.

Gray nuzzled her neck before moving down to sniff at her leg. She wanted to assure him that she would be fine, but she was just too tired. There was no way she'd be able to shift. The air around her swirled as Gray began the change back to human form. Beth watched him, amazed that he was still able to change back and forth with all the adrenaline in his body. That couldn't have felt good.

"Hey, you're going to be okay." He ran his hands gently up and down her sides. He glanced up at Dawson. "Julian? Claude and Dorothy?"

"Everyone's all right," Dawson called back.

"Do we need an ambulance?" Joe asked joining Gray.

Beth shook her head. She didn't want to waste the time going to the clinic in town when she'd heal on her own.

"I'm going to take her to my room," Gray said. "Let her rest and check for other injuries. Do you need help with the three felines?"

"No," Joe said. "You go ahead. We'll take care of everything out here."

Gray was careful when he picked her up, cradling her in his arms, but it still jostled her and she couldn't hold in a hiss.

"Sorry," he said, wincing.

She nodded back.

"Is Aunt Beth going to be okay?" Julian asked when Gray stepped onto the deck.

"Yes," Gray told the boy. "She's just really tired. She'll be just fine."

"I was so scared. But Aunt Beth wasn't. She was brave," Julian said, his lower lip trembling.

Gray crouched, which couldn't have been easy still holding Beth. "Can I tell you a secret?"

Julian bobbed his head as he scooted closer to them.

"I was scared, and I bet if your aunt could talk right now, she'd tell you that she'd been as well. It's okay to be frightened when put in a bad situation," Gray said quietly.

"Really?" Julian's eyes were wide and glassy.

Beth licked his check.

Julian laughed as Gray chuckled.

"Yes, really," Gray assured him. "Now, how about you help me?"

"Okay!" Julian stood up. "What can I do?"

"I'm going to take your aunt upstairs," Gray said. "Can you open the doors for me?"

"I can," Julian replied quickly. He ran off to the front of the inn.

Gray rose then stepped over to Dorothy and Claude. "You two sure you're okay?" he asked.

"Dorothy has a small bump on the back of her head, but I don't think it's too bad," Claude said. "I'm going to take her to the clinic just to be sure, though."

"Good idea," Gray agreed.

"I'll keep an eye on things here for you," Dawson said.

"Let me know if you need any help," Gray told Dawson. "I'll be upstairs with Beth."

"You got it," Dawson replied.

As Gray carried her toward the entrance, Beth gazed up at him. He'd come for her, for them, and she didn't ever want him not to be there. It didn't matter what she needed to do. Beth had fallen in love with the wolf shifter. Their future was together and Beth needed to confess that to him.

It was time to take a chance.

Even if that meant leaving everyone else she loved behind.

Chapter Eight

Gray sat quietly in a chair next to his bed where Beth was sleeping peacefully. It had been two hours since he'd come across the heart-stopping sight of Beth facing off against an enraged tiger and he'd barely finished shaking.

It had taken him until that moment to realize what he'd already known deep down—Beth was the woman he would spend the rest of his life with.

In less than a week, he'd gone from feeling alone and lost to becoming completely smitten. There was always the possibility that he was about to make the biggest mistake of his life, but Gray was going to have to take that gamble.

He would not be leaving Coyote Bluff.

Somehow, some way, Gray was going to have to figure out how to make a life in the town. He had no idea what he would do, but the only thing that mattered was that he'd found a home he hadn't even known he'd been searching for.

A soft knock interrupted his thoughts and he jumped up to head to the door before whoever it was woke Beth.

"Hey, Gray," RJ said as Gray cracked open the door. "I was just checking on the two of you."

Gray slipped into the hall, closing the door quietly behind him. "She shifted back during her sleep, not even waking. She's worn-out but already healing."

"That's good." RJ tilted his head toward the railing. "Got a minute?"

"Sure." Curious, he followed RJ across the hall until they were braced on the wooden banister. They could see the bottom floor of the inn. Everything was currently quiet, but

Gray could smell something delicious cooking. "What's up?"

"It's time for me to join my brother," RJ said. "Now that everyone involved in kidnapping the Prince has been found, I have to go."

"I understand," Gray said. "You have to be there to support your brother. It won't be easy for him to go into an established Pack as the new Alpha."

"Yeah." RJ nodded. "He's already meeting some resistance."

"If you need anything at all, you give me a call," Gray offered.

"I was going to tell you the same thing," RJ stated.

Gray raised an eyebrow.

"You're staying here, aren't you?" RJ asked.

"Yes," Gray admitted out loud for the first time. "I'm staying in Coyote Bluff and hopefully with Beth."

"I don't think you'll have any issues here. Coyote Bluff is an amazingly accepting, but if you get trouble from anyone or anywhere else, you let me know. My new Pack is only a few hours from here and I've got your back."

It stunned him that he'd started off fighting the other man and now felt a solid bond that would last a lifetime. Gray nodded then pulled RJ into a back-slapping hug.

"Keep in touch," Gray told RJ.

"Of course, brother," RJ replied. "And I expect you to bring your woman up as soon as things get settled."

"It's a promise." RJ strolled down the stairs until he disappeared through the front door.

It appeared that things were changing for a lot of them. With Casey's team ending their service, they had decisions of their own to make about their futures. Gray hoped he'd still be able to see them now that he had connected to the family.

A few minutes after RJ had walked out, the front door reopened and Julian came running through. The boy didn't notice Gray up above and that gave him a few moments to just watch. It wouldn't be easy leaving Jesse behind. He'd been with her and Tyler since she'd been born and Gray considered himself an uncle. He knew that Jesse also thought of him that way. But this was his chance to maybe have a child of his own. Beth's affection for the boy was obvious. He'd like to see her with a baby of her own.

Julian skipped into the dining room, going out of view. Gray turned back to his bedroom. He quietly re-entered, but as soon as the door closed behind him, Beth started to stir.

She rolled over onto her side, rising to peer at him. "Everything okay?" she asked.

"Fine," Gray assured her. "RJ was just saying goodbye."

"Oh. I guess it's really over now. Everyone's going to have to carry on with their own lives."

Here was his moment. Gray strode over to sit on the side of the mattress closest to her. "Not everyone."

"What do you mean?" She sat up, putting her back against the headboard.

"I'm not leaving," he declared.

She nodded. "You said you'd stay a couple of days. Your Alpha is giving you some time off."

Gray smiled then took her hand in his. "I mean, I'm not leaving at all. I want to stay in Coyote Bluff."

"What?" she asked softly.

Fuck, that wasn't the reaction he'd expected. Even if Beth didn't feel the same way as he did, Gray still had faith that they would end up together and he was okay with spending the time to convince her. "I'm not leaving. I want to make Coyote Bluff my home."

"Gray." She kneeled in front of him on the mattress. "Say it again."

"I'm not leaving. I want to make Coyote Bluff my home."

Beth smiled so sweetly that Gray's hope spiked. "What if I'm willing to go with you? Would that change your decision?"

"You'd move to Colorado?" he asked.

"I've been thinking about it," she admitted. "I'm not ready to let you go. If you have to leave, then I want to go with you."

Not only was Beth at the same place as he was for their future, but she'd be giving up everything she loved to join him. Gray couldn't let her do that. Coyote Bluff was her home and they'd already received support from the residents.

Gray wanted to believe that his Pack would accept whoever he picked as a mate, but he couldn't guarantee it. There was no doubt in his mind that Tyler and his good friends were going to be happy for him, but not every member of the Pack was going to understand his choice of a feline shifter.

Beth deserved to be comfortable in her home. There would be too many uncertainties and doubts for Gray to back with him.

"Can I be honest?" he asked. Gray didn't want to hurt her feelings, but they should make this decision together.

"Yes," she replied quickly. "Please."

"If we were to go to Colorado, I wouldn't want it to be right away. We already have people here that will support us."

"You don't think your Pack will want me." She didn't say it as a question.

"Tyler will and he'd demand the same from his Pack, but no Pack is perfect. If I can't assure myself you'd be safe, I won't take the chance."

"We might have issues here," she pointed out.

"Yes," Gray said. "But with the different species living peacefully, I think we'll find more acceptance. In a Pack of wolf shifters, you're going to stand out all the time."

"I'll admit I'm relieved," she told him.

"You are?"

"I don't want to leave my brother or nephew. This town is the first place that I felt a connection to and bonded with. I really would love to stay."

He'd known he was making the right decision. Beth's admission helped ease his mind even more. "Maybe we'll be able to visit, but I want us to plan our future here."

"I'm so happy!" Beth cried, wrapping her arms around his neck.

Gray didn't actually need to hear the words, but it was nice all the same. She was peppering his neck with kisses, but Gray was already beginning to feel a more powerful need.

"Lie back," he said while gently nudging her to comply.

Beth peered up at him with all the love and affection he felt toward her.

"Let me show you how good it can be between us," he offered.

"I already know," she told him. "I just want more."

"You'll have it," he promised. Gray tugged his shirt over his head then leaned down to tease her lips with his tongue.

When she pushed up to increase the pressure, Gray nipped her bottom lip.

Beth laughed but laid her head back down on the pillow. Gray slid his hand down her shoulder to cup her breasts. Thankfully she was already naked from falling asleep as a bobcat. He could admire her body tonight and for so much longer now.

She arched, thrusting her chest into his hold, but he didn't pull back this time. Instead he leaned forward, taking one pert nipple into his mouth and sucking. Beth cried out, her hands going to the back of his head. Gray licked a path down, lavishing attention on her soft skin. He loved how fully she gave herself to him.

As she spread her thighs, allowing him to settle comfortably between her legs, he rewarded her with a brush of his thumbs back over her nipples.

Already she was starting to flush. Gray wanted her desperately.

He sat back on his heels then rubbed his fingers through her folds so he could feel the wetness. She wanted him just as much, but still wasn't that desperate.

Gray dropped down, pinning her under his larger body to bury his face in her sweet pussy.

"Gray!" she called out.

He hummed but didn't stop the erotic torment of licking at her entrance while rubbing his thumb over her clit.

"Please! More!" she demanded.

Almost there. Gray slid his palms under her ass and lifted her to give him better access. He tongued her open, collecting the juices of her essence before plunging in to get a deeper taste.

She trembled for him.

"Gray!" Beth climaxed but Gray didn't pause, didn't stop until she tugged his hair so hard he worried that she'd yanked some out.

He climbed up and positioned himself to enter her. Gray waited until she opened her eyes and reached for him before thrusting hard. The bed rocked with them, but he wasn't done making the furniture move. With a good grip of her hips, he withdrew then plunged back. Repeating the action over and over.

Beth lifted her legs to brace them under his arms which opened her farther for every powerful drive. Pumping his hips as fast as he could, Gray felt every part of his soul needing to claim Beth as his.

He wouldn't, of course. There'd be a serious conversation before he mated with her, but now he knew one day the option was available. Gray needed Beth, always would, and he had to show her. Every damn day.

"Gray," she moaned. The way she clawed at his back both turned him on and made it hard to concentrate on loving her. If she didn't stop, he was going to lose control.

"Fuck!" he snarled. Her sweet cunt clamped down on him. He jerked her hips even harder against his groin before plowing on.

His orgasm built.

Gray knew he couldn't handle any more.

"Yes!" He plunged deep one last time before he came. Beth was still lifting her hips, forcing his cock deep. Then she heaved at his shoulders, shoved him back and climbed on top.

Beth grasped his cock and positioned him at her entrance before slamming herself down. Gray could only lie there gasping as she used his body for her own pleasure. And he loved every moment of it.

When he had more control, Gray cupped her breasts while she rode him.

Gazing up at her, he was amazed by her beauty and the fact she'd deemed him good enough for her.

Gray was in heaven.

* * * *

The fact that someone was once again banging on his door made Gray realize he was going to have to figure out a more permanent living situation. Even though Beth was snuggled into his arms, if whoever was outside didn't go away, he was going to kill them.

After the day we had yesterday, don't I deserve to sleep in? The pounding came again and he sighed before slipping his arm from under Beth's head.

"Tell whoever is at the door that I plan on killing them," she mumbled.

Gray peered down and had to smile. She was just so adorable ruffled and sleepy-eyed. "I'll do that." He placed a quick kiss to her forehead before climbing off the mattress. While tempted to answer naked just to be a dick, Gray stopped to pull on a pair of boxers.

He stomped to the door and threw it open before realizing his mistake. He hadn't connected the scent of home until he was staring at his Alpha, who had two people behind him.

"What?" he managed.

"Jesus Christ!" Kiley pushed past Tyler and was in Gray's arms before he even knew what was happening. "We were so worried."

Out of habit, he'd caught Kiley who clung to him, but he looked at his Alpha before turning to Kiley's mate, Austin. "Huh?"

"Uh, Gray?" Beth called. "Why is another woman climbing you?"

Kiley stiffened before doing a slow scan of the room. He knew the minute she caught sight of Beth in his bed. Kiley shifted back then he was shoved forcefully toward Tyler as Kiley planted her hands on her hips.

Shit, fuck, damn... this is bad.

"Who are you?" Kiley asked quite rudely.

To her credit, Beth merely smiled. "Kiley?"

Obviously taken back, Kiley glared at him before nodding.

"And the other two men must be Gray's Alpha and your mate?" Beth guessed.

"You sure seem to know a lot about us," Kiley stated. She stalked forward before Gray had a chance to grab her arm. "All I know about you is that you shared a bed with my best friend."

"Kiley!" Gray snapped. He didn't care how much he loved his friend — no one spoke to Beth that way.

Beth arranged the blankets high but smiled at him. "It's okay, Gray."

"It is not!" Kiley exclaimed. "Since he's been in this happy little town, he's been attacked twice. The last time we don't even hear about from him. Then he doesn't answer his phone for over twenty-four hours! Things are far from okay."

"Twenty-four hours?" Gray and Beth said at the same time.

"Kiley." Austin stepped farther into the room. He shot Gray an apologetic smile, but Gray knew he was lucky Kiley had even allowed them to knock on the door. Kiley was able and willing to use some of her more questionable skills from being a private detective when it suited her. "Maybe we should let Gray and..."

"Beth!" Gray said. "Her name is Beth and what the hell are you three doing here?"

Out of everyone, Gray didn't expect it to be Beth who began to laugh uncontrollably. After a minute, Tyler and Austin joined her. That left him and Kiley peering at the weirdos around them.

"Damn it!" Gray threw his hands in the air. "What's so funny?"

Kiley snorted. "Okay, looking at this from your point of view, this is kind of funny," Kiley said to Beth.

Beth nodded, wiping her eyes.

"How about the two of you get dressed and join us downstairs? I'm fucking starving and I swear I smelled steak," Kiley said.

"Sounds good," Beth agreed easily.

Kiley spun toward him. "You better hurry up. I think we make your hosts nervous."

Gray had no doubt that Dorothy and Claude were more than a little nervous with so many wolf shifters around. They'd been wary when he'd arrived alone but now the number of wolves was multiplying. He'd also bet that Dawson had already been informed of his Alpha's visit. "We won't be long."

Kiley pressed her lips together into a thin line then stalked out, grabbing his mate's arms as she went.

Tyler shook his head. "I'm sorry. I didn't even think anything about bringing her. I was telling Austin what had been going on and she overheard. Austin couldn't do anything to keep her home. It was either come with her or be responsible for what she did once she arrived."

"I know," Gray smiled. "I am really glad to see you, though. Hell, I'm happy to see her and Austin." He threw a glance over his shoulder at Beth. "A little warning would have been nice."

"I tried calling," Tyler said. "Kiley called. Austin called. Several others."

"Sorry." Gray hadn't meant to worry anyone. "I don't

even know how long we've been asleep."

"As long as you're okay." Tyler dipped his head in respect to Beth. "But I do think the two of you should hurry. Now that we know you're unharmed, there's no telling what trouble Kiley will find."

Gray watched his Alpha turn and leave before he closed the door. He braced himself for whatever reaction Beth was going to have.

Beth had her phone in her hand. "I have ten missed calls. We slept all day yesterday and half of today."

"You needed your rest," he said.

She raised an eyebrow.

"Okay, we both did," Gray admitted. "But, fuck, I am so sorry about this."

Beth cocked her head to the side. "About what?"

"Kiley and the others busting in on us."

"You're happy to see them," she commented.

He was. Gray had planned to call Tyler and explain that he wouldn't be returning, but now he would also have to deal with Kiley. "Kiley's harmless."

Beth scoffed.

"She will be," Gray corrected. "We've been friends a long time."

"You already told me about her," Beth said. "And it's obvious that the two of you still adore each other. But even I can tell that Austin is completely in love with her and I have the feeling that she feels the same way."

"Yes," he agreed.

"Then you need to relax. Enjoy their visit," Beth told him. "Are you going to talk to Tyler while he's here?"

"Yes," Gray said. "Although I'd like to do it without Kiley around. She just left us, which was hard for Tyler and Jesse. I don't want him to feel abandoned by me too."

"I could take Kiley and her mate around town. Show them the community," Beth offered. "That would give you some time alone with your Alpha."

"You'd do that?"

"I want to," she said. "You have to remember that I get to keep you after this. Anything I can do to make things easier for you, I will."

Gray walked over to the bed and pulled her up to kiss her thoroughly. "You are the best," he said. "If Kiley starts to get annoying, bring up kids. Nothing will get her to shut up as fast as that."

Beth laughed loudly. "That's mean!"

"Hey! A guy's gotta learn some tricks," he defended. "She can probably kick the ass of most male shifters I know."

"I'm actually looking forward to spending time with her," Beth said. "She's important to you, so I want to be friends."

"Oh, you will be," Gray said. "I have no doubt. But we have to go save Claude and Dorothy."

"Let me brush my teeth," Beth rushed off.

Gray decided to go casual. If Beth managed to get Kiley away, he'd like to shift with his Alpha. Having Tyler in wolf form was always so comforting. And Gray didn't know when he'd get the chance again. He grabbed a clean pair of faded jeans and a plain navy shirt. By having dressed quickly, he'd finished by the time Beth exited the bathroom. They switched places so she could pull on clothing while he took care of his morning routine.

It couldn't have taken them more than ten minutes, but Gray still grew nervous as he and Beth followed the sound of voices into the dining room. Gray paused in the doorway, making Beth almost run into his back.

Kiley was crouched facing Julian, who was speaking animatedly to her. Tyler, Austin and Dawson sat at one of the bigger tables, drinking what appeared to be coffee.

"The dead have arisen," Dawson called, spotting them.

Gray refused to be embarrassed. He'd been on the hunt for a long time and since he'd arrived in Coyote Bluff it'd been nonstop chaos.

"Gray!" Julian yelled. He ran at Gray, who scooped him up.

"What's up, little man?" he asked.

146

"She's a lady wolf!" Julian pointed at Kiley.

"I know," Gray said. "She's my friend."

"She's the only one who didn't promise not to eat me," Julian tattled.

Gray whipped his head toward Kiley.

"What?" she snapped. "I'm not going to lie to the kid."

"She's not going to eat you," Gray told Julian.

"Not unless I do something really bad," Julian said.

"Kiley!" Gray couldn't believe that she'd even joked about that.

"In her defense," Dawson spoke up, "she was totally blindsided by my boy."

"I'm keeping my eye on him," Kiley warned. "I think he might work for the secret service or something."

Julian giggled.

He didn't even know what to say. Gray peered at Beth for help, but she was shaking with laughter. He growled before strolling over to the table. He sat down as far from Kiley as he could. Maybe Gray should be more worried about Kiley and Julian. She would be a terrible influence on the boy. Julian didn't need any help getting into trouble.

Still, Gray could see how well his family would mesh with the residents in Coyote Bluff. There was absolutely no reason he'd have to stop seeing his pack when he moved permanently. He just needed to tell Tyler.

Tyler sat across from him and when Gray glanced at his Alpha, he was surprised by the expression on Tyler's face. His Alpha was peering at him with affection but somehow also sadness. When Tyler dipped his head slightly, Gray had the feeling that he wasn't going to have to explain too much. Tyler already knew.

"I was really starting to worry about the two of you," Dorothy said as she bustled into the room carrying a tray. Claude was walking behind her and smiled at Gray as well.

Dorothy set her tray on an empty table then bent to kiss his cheek before doing the same to Beth. "I thought you might have been more hurt than we'd known."

"Just tired," Gray assured the older woman. "We're up and ready for adventure. What're you doing later? Is there a drug house or something in town that needs taking down?"

Dawson and Claude groaned while everyone else laughed.

"I think you can take a few more days off before you go back to cleaning up the streets of Coyote Bluff," Dorothy said, swatting him.

"Billy Jefferies stole my gummy bears last week," Julian piped up.

Gray glanced down at the boy and bared his teeth. "You just point him out to me."

Julian giggled, nodding.

"Now, Gray," Kiley admonished. "You know you can't go picking on little boys. Julian can tell me. No one knows me here."

"Okay!" Julian jumped down and raced over to Kiley's side.

Gray reached for the kid, missed his arm and grunted. This was not a good idea. Beth patting his hand had him looking at her for help.

"We have to keep him away from the she-devil," he mock-whispered.

"I can hear you," Kiley singsonged. "And I can stay longer than a few days if you're not nice."

Gray shuddered dramatically.

"You behave," Dorothy scolded. She set down a mug of coffee and a full plate of breakfast food. He noticed that Beth received the same, but the others were eating full plates of dinner food. He nodded toward his plate. "You haven't eaten in over a day. Let's take it easy for now. I want to make sure you're not coming down sick."

Emotion choked him up. Gray caught Dorothy's hand and gave it a gentle squeeze. He wasn't certain he could express in words what he was feeling.

No one took care of him anymore. It was his job to stand in front of the pack and while his fellow wolf shifters had his back and wouldn't let him get hurt, no one mothered him.

Claude laid his palm over Gray and Dorothy's, shocking Gray further.

Maybe he wouldn't be so quick to move out of the inn. Gray couldn't see himself living in Coyote Bluff and not visiting with the older couple daily. Plus Claude's dominance soothed his wolf side, which needed to have a strong leader around. Claude would never be Gray's Alpha, but he was something.

"Eat, son," Claude mumbled. "Then you can enjoy time with your friends. Leave your worry for now."

Gray nodded and picked up his fork. With his free hand, he reached for Beth's fingers beneath the table. He could follow that order. Claude was right. He didn't need to worry. Gray had made up his mind and he was now going to be part of the Coyote Bluff community.

Beth didn't know where Dawson, Austin or Julian had disappeared to but she was pretty certain that it'd been planned. Sitting on the back deck of the inn with beers, she found herself alone with Kiley for the first time.

The sun had already begun to set, so it was a pretty sight, but the longer Kiley sat there without speaking, the more nervous Beth grew. She wanted this woman who was so important to Gray to like her. Finally she'd had enough.

"I figured you'd start your interrogation," Beth stated.

Kiley glanced over and smiled. "I'd planned to, but the view sort of took my breath away. I wouldn't have ever guessed that the canyons would look so astounding. It's quite beautiful."

Beth beamed. Kiley wasn't saying anything positive about her, but it still felt like her approval of Beth's town meant something.

"But now that you've brought it up, I guess we should talk," Kiley said.

"Should have kept my trap shut," Beth mumbled.

"It'll be painless, I promise."

Beth noticed for the first time how tense Kiley was. With her own anxiety so high, Beth hadn't thought about how awkward this would be for the other woman. "I'm not going to hurt him. That's what you want to hear, but I'm not just saying it, I mean it."

Kiley shook her head. "I think being mated to Austin changed me."

"How?"

"Instead of worrying about Gray getting hurt, I'm trying to figure out a way to let him go. He belongs to you now," Kiley said.

"You don't have to let him go completely," Beth told her. "I don't want to keep the two of you apart. I just want to have a part of him, too."

"You have more than just a part of him," Kiley said. She gazed back out toward the canyons. "He's staying, isn't he?"

"Yes." Beth didn't think any more words than that were necessary.

"I figured. The way he looks at you is how Austin's always looked at me. The minute I saw the two of you together, I knew."

"Knew what?" Beth asked carefully.

"That he loves you."

Beth smiled. She couldn't help it. Someone else could see the things she saw when she looked at Gray. It wasn't just her imagination.

"I think this is a good place for him as well," Kiley said.

"Really?" Beth was truly shocked by that.

"Gray's the type who needs to help. Has to feel useful. If the shifters announce their presence, there'll be a need to protect all of you in this town," Kiley said. "Gray will bring the protection of the Pack, but he'll also fight to keep everyone safe. It's almost the perfect place for him."

"I can't see anyone here wanting to be a part of that," Beth admitted.

"No, I didn't think they would. But Tyler told me that your older brother is mated to the Prince of felines. Keeping this town a secret will benefit him as well giving him a retreat from the outside world. Also making Coyote Bluff need Gray even more."

"I guess I haven't thought about things like that," Beth admitted.

"Gray has. And I have a feeling Tyler has as well. I think he knew before we even got here."

"Will he try to talk Gray into leaving?" Beth asked. She couldn't hold in the concern and Kiley had been honest with her. Surely Kiley had some sort of idea how the Alpha would react.

"No. Tyler loves Gray, but he always does what's best for the individual. I wasn't actually part of the Pack, so it wasn't a big deal for me to leave. Tyler still calls me every other day. It helps that Austin is his best friend, but you shouldn't expect any different. In fact you might want to start preparing for a massive increase in visits, because I suspect someone from the Pack will be around most of the time."

"Why?" Beth exclaimed. Having an increase of wolf shifters was going to affect everyone in town.

"Because you and your community will be a part of Gray's family. He's already bonding with you all. There is no way Tyler or any of us will leave Gray or you on your own."

"I don't know quite what to say." She didn't know how to feel, either.

"It won't be to take over anything." Kiley looked at Beth as she spoke. "I don't think Claude would allow it, anyway."

"You haven't met the sheriff, either," Beth said. "Between the two of them, they keep other shifters from trying to dominate here."

"Good," Kiley said. "It's about the bond with wolf shifters. Gray will still need that."

"I'll admit I don't know much about your species."

Kiley waved her hand. "We're pretty simple. Most of what

Gray needs he'll get through you and the other connections he's made here. But there will be times when he'll need a fellow wolf. It's instinctual, but if anyone can make it work it'll be Gray and Tyler. You should just be prepared. We're a nosy group."

Beth laughed. "I don't think I've seen the last of RJ or Mike, either."

"The wolves who served with your brother?"

"Yeah, they were pretty crazy, but they seemed to have bonded with Gray as well."

"You both have a lot of people on your side."

"I think so," Beth replied. "Gray still believes that we'll get some trouble from shifters who won't understand a wolf and bobcat together."

"What do you think?"

"I don't know," Beth answered honestly.

"Wolf culture is a little different than felines and if there are problems, it will probably come from our kind. But, like I said, you have a lot of people who'll have your back. Plus your brother is mated to the fucking Prince. Anyone would be stupid to mess with you."

"So you don't mind?"

"Not at all," Kiley assured her. "I think it's perfect."

Beth relaxed in her chair. She brought her beer to her lips and ignored the fact she'd allowed it to get warm. Now that she could relax, she wanted to enjoy sitting out with her new friend.

Kiley must have felt the same way since she slouched in her chair, taking a deep breath. Beth didn't know how the other woman could be mated to an Alpha. As much as she loved Gray, she was so thankful he wasn't in charge of an entire Pack. That had to put a strain on things. Instead Beth could continue to care for her family and live her own life.

A life with Gray by her side.

Chapter Nine

Gray glanced around the inn's backyard, looking for Beth. He found her lounging in the grass with Julian, Kiley and Jesse. The four of them had quickly become close. In just three days, Gray had already seen a calendar brought out numerous times, scheduling visits between Coyote Bluff, Tyler's territory and Austin and Kiley's. He foresaw a lot of traveling in his future.

The fact that just three days after he'd told Tyler he was staying in Coyote Bluff his Alpha and Kiley had organized all this was amazing. They'd already made certain Gray had some of his belongings as well as several friendly faces from home, and that meant the world to him.

"Great party," Tyler told him, coming up and handing him a beer. "I'm a little surprised that our hosts could pull something like this together so fast. I don't think even I could have done it."

Gray grinned at him. "It is what they do for a living."

Claude and Dorothy were the absolute best. They hadn't balked at his request to host some of the Pack as his friends brought down some of his stuff. Instead, they'd made it a celebration. Everyone who had arrived in town had simply fallen in love with the community and the people, just like Gray had done. And no one had eaten Julian, either.

He chuckled at the memory of Julian's face when all the wolves had started showing up. But, as children do, Julian had made instant friends with everyone. Jesse, Tyler's daughter, had declared him the most awesome cat ever. He couldn't wait to see what would happen once those two were actually able to shift.

"You seem happy," Tyler pointed out.

Gray gazed around. "I am. I really am. Even though I don't know what is going to happen I feel like I made the right choice staying here."

"I agree. I was going to tell you that you would always be a member of the Pack. Always welcome, both you and Beth. The longer I spend here, I see I don't need to."

Gray looked at him. "No?"

"I can see your Pack is here now," Tyler pronounced with a smile at the crowd and hugged Gray close. "Maybe it'll be an extension of your old one or might be a different branch of a tree, but this community is as much as your pack as we've ever been."

"You'll still always be my family," Gray whispered to his best friend. God, the two of them had been through so much together. It would be so weird not to see Tyler every day.

Tyler slapped him on the back. "Oh, I know — you'll not get rid of us that easy. I have a pretty big job for you as well."

"You do?" he questioned warily. Gray wasn't ready to go on any more missions. He wanted — no, needed — to spend time in his new community. It was time for him to settle down and enjoy his life.

"Do you see the man sitting under the tree at the edge of the property?" Tyler asked.

Gray practically had to squint. The inn's yard was huge and with all the added guests plus most of the town folk, it wasn't easy to see who Tyler was talking about. But yes, he could see a smaller guy around his own age. Gray definitely hadn't met him yet. "Who is he?"

"That is the only other wolf shifter in town. His name is Mark Brier," Tyler said.

"Oh." Gray didn't know what to say. Beth had barely told him anything about Mark when he'd asked her. She had promised to introduce Gray, though, if she got the chance. Beth was friends with the quiet wolf shifter, but she also wanted Mark to bond with his own species as well.

"That's where I went this morning after breakfast," Tyler told him.

"To meet with a strange wolf shifter without back-up?" Gray growled. What in the hell had his Alpha been thinking?

Tyler smiled. "I'm an Alpha. I wasn't in any danger."

"Maybe not from him, but what if he had friends? There might still be blow-back from the problems with the felines."

"I appreciate your concern, but I was asked to do a favor by the Council and it needed to be handled alone," Tyler said.

Well shit. If the Council was getting involved, Gray really needed to figure out what was going on. "What do you need from me?"

"Just talk to him," Tyler advised.

"Talk?" Gray scoffed. There had to be more to the request.

"Mark has been through some hard times," Tyler told him. "He's been in a situation worse than Kiley's. All his life he's struggled to fit in and be accepted. The Council finally got him out of a horrible circumstance but he bailed before they could find a Pack for him. They've tried numerous times to have him meet with Alphas, but Mark always refuses."

"Then what can I do? I'm not an Alpha."

"Exactly," Tyler said. "You can talk to him and treat him like another wolf shifter. He's a really nice man, shy and quiet, but smart and funny. I think the two of you'd be great friends."

"The Council wants a spy?" Gray wouldn't do it. If Mark was hiding out in Coyote Bluff then he had his reasons. Gray would not betray the younger man.

"No," Tyler assured him. "They want another wolf who will protect him. Mark's left his past behind, but we all know that doesn't always mean he'll stay safe. The Council wants Mark to be able to turn to someone, anyone really, but another wolf would be ideal. If Mark runs into trouble, we need to have his back. They fear that he'd run and disappear rather than tell anyone he needs assistance."

That didn't sound so bad. "I'll talk to him," Gray said. "Beth is already friendly with him and I'd like to get to know him as well. As long as the Council doesn't expect me to report back, I'll keep an eye on things."

"Thank you." Tyler patted his shoulder. "I knew you would do it whether or not we asked, but I also wanted you to be aware that you might not be completely out of danger, even here."

"I appreciate the heads-up." Gray peered round the yard once again. With so many different species talking, laughing and visiting with one another, it still struck him as weird. His entire life had been spent with his own kind. Every once in a while, he might have crossed paths with another species, but for the most part he'd always imagined settling down with a fellow wolf shifter and protecting his Alpha.

"Don't think too hard," Tyler advised.

"About what?" Gray asked, but he knew Tyler was easily figuring out the direction Gray's mind was going.

"I've only been around you a few days and I can tell Beth is perfect for you."

"She is," Gray stated with confidence. "But I wonder if being with me is best for her."

"Why would you even think that?"

"I don't know much about felines," he admitted. "And really my experience with the few I've met hasn't always ended up good. I'm scared I won't be able to give Beth something she needs. I can't provide for her if I don't know what's missing."

"And this is why I told you not to think so hard about it." Tyler gripped his shoulder then led him farther away from the others. "Do you want to be with Beth?"

"More than anything," Gray told him. "That's why I'm turning my entire life upside down."

"Then listen to me." Tyler stepped in front of Gray, which was a little intimidating. Tyler wasn't mad at him, but having his Alpha close to his face instinctively had Gray wanting to drop his gaze.

"You're a human first," Tyler said quietly. "Yes, we have the animal sides of ourselves, but you don't let the wolf rule your actions. Be the man that you have always been and everything is going to work out fine. Beth is going to tell you what she wants and needs."

"I know." Gray took a deep breath before blowing it out slowly. "I know that. It's just my nerves, I think. Everything is changing."

"Do you remember what you told me when I was offered the position to take over for Riker?"

Gray smiled. "When something is meant to be, it'll happen."

"You've found your place here," Tyler said. "It might not be where you thought you'd end up, but I wouldn't leave you here if I didn't think you belonged. If I was worried, I'd do whatever I had to in order to get you back home."

That made Gray feel better. He wasn't even sure why. "Thanks, Alpha."

"Of course. Now I'm going to get some food. You need to mingle with your new community."

Gray knew he was lucky as he watched his Alpha walk away. After what had seemed like forever, he'd finally found his mate and a new home. Joe had offered him a job with the sheriff's office, which Gray had gladly accepted. There might not have been a lot of crime in Coyote Bluff, but Gray was determined to keep his new community safe.

Which meant he did need to get to know the residents of Coyote Bluff. Spotting the lone wolf shifter again, Gray strode forward. Maybe it would be best to talk to Mark without anyone else around.

He was aware the moment that the younger shifter spotted him heading in his direction. Mark stiffened before placing his head down.

"Hey!" Gray called from several yards away. He didn't want to intimate Mark.

"Hello," Mark replied quietly.

Keeping his gaze on Mark's shoulder, Gray slowed until he was a few feet away. "I wanted to introduce myself." He crouched so he wasn't towering over Mark. Leaning forward just enough that they could touch, Gray offered his hand. "I'm Gray."

Mark didn't flinch from him, which was a good sign. "Mark."

"Mind if I sit for a minute?" Gray asked once they'd shaken hands. Mark's palm was soft and the hold had no strength behind it. Gray would have to work to help Mark with his confidence.

Mark shrugged his skinny shoulders.

Gray sat, making certain that there was plenty of space between the two of them. If Mark wanted to run, Gray wouldn't stop him. "I think Beth was going to introduce us later, but I thought I'd come over and say hi. It didn't look like you were enjoying yourself much."

The way the backyard was laid out, Mark was under a tree at the top of a small hill. With Gray sitting closer to the other guests, he'd put himself lower than Mark, giving the younger shifter the position of power. Mark probably didn't realize it, but Gray hoped the wolf part of him would.

"Thanks for coming out," Gray said. He needed to start some sort of conversation. "I guess it's probably not your thing, but I know Beth appreciates it."

"I promised her," Mark told him. "Beth is sweet. I try not to disappoint her if I can help it."

"Good." Gray grinned. "Got any tips for me? I'm pretty sure there is a dog house in her backyard and I'd prefer not to sleep in it."

Mark chuckled then slapped a hand over his mouth.

"Nah, man," Gray said. "It's funny. True but funny. I've never been in a serious relationship like this before so I'm bound to mess up. Maybe she'll at least give me a pillow."

Mark nodded, still wide-eyed.

"My fur should keep me warm on those nights," Gray

continued to joke.

"There's some —"

Gray waited for Mark to continue, but the younger shifter had dropped his head, hiding his blush.

"Some what?" Gray asked softly. "Come on, man, you gotta help me out. Us wolves have to stick together."

Mark's head snapped up. "You wouldn't say that if you knew me."

Now they were getting somewhere. Gray didn't want to push Mark into revealing something he wasn't ready to, but if Mark wanted to talk, Gray would listen.

"I don't know." Gray leaned back, spreading out his arms to hold himself up. "I've met a lot of wolf shifters. Some of them have been great and some are complete bastards. I think I'm pretty good at reading people and you seem like a decent guy. Beth cares about you, so I know I can trust you."

Mark snorted.

"I mean it," Gray said. "If you'll give me a chance, I think we'll be good friends."

"Really?" Mark threw him a glance. He was clenching his fists. "Friends?"

"Why not?"

"Maybe we can even shift together?" Mark pressed.

"Sure."

"This is a fucking joke." Mark moved like he was going to stand.

"Wait!" Gray held his palms up. "What did I say?"

This time when Mark leaned forward, Gray could see the fury on his eyes. "You just came over here to fuck with me."

"No," Gray replied slowly. "I did not." It was obvious that Gray had missed something big. It wasn't fair having no idea what was going on.

"I'm deformed!" Mark practically shouted.

"Oh." Gray glanced around, thankful that no one seemed to be paying attention to them. "I'm sorry. Can you not shift? That's okay. We can find something else to do."

"Are you being serious right now?" Mark snapped.

"Yes." Gray nodded solemnly. "I didn't know. I obviously brought up a sore subject and I apologize."

"I can shift. I just don't like to in front of anyone... It's not been good for other shifters to see me like that."

"Shit!" Gray could only imagine how Mark's Pack must have treated him. He'd had an idea of abuse, but this went much further.

"Exactly," Mark stated.

"But if you wanted to transform and run with someone, I'd still be willing."

Mark shook his head. "You might not be an Alpha, but you're still pretty dominant. I'd prefer to avoid another beating."

"I wouldn't do that!" Gray exclaimed. "I'm not like that."

"It's instinct," Mark responded. The expression on his face spoke volumes. The young shifter actually believed that.

"No," Gray assured him. "If you were told that then it was by some assholes. A true Pack mate would never attack you for being different. No matter if you're deformed, weaker or sick. That is not how your Pack should have treated you. Especially an Alpha or dominant wolf."

"Even my parents treated me like a freak," Mark shared. "They were actually some of the worst."

Fuck, Gray couldn't resist. He scooted closer to Mark and placed his hand on the young shifter's knee. "Never again," he declared. "Whether we decide to be friends or not, I won't let anyone be treated like that in front of me."

Mark smiled sadly. He tilted his head to peer across the yard but didn't move away from Gray. "I think about the kids here. Some of them will be shifting soon. I often wonder what will happen if something is wrong with their shifted form."

"If there is, then we'll support and care of that shifter," Gray said. "Maybe your experience will help someone else."

"That's what the Council tells me," Mark said. "I don't want to go from Pack to Pack and share what happened. I just want to be left alone. I like it here. I have enough privacy that I don't feel caged in, but I'm not alone."

"I understand," Gray replied. "I'll do whatever I can to get the Council off your back. You just tell me what you need and I'll do my best."

"Why would you do that?" You don't even know me."

"I would do it for anyone or any species," Gray said. "At least I hope I would. I'm lucky enough that I was raised by and with some of the most compassionate shifters. I volunteered to help search for the feline Prince. I want to pay back some of the fortune I've been blessed with."

Mark didn't say anything for a minute and the silence stretched on, but Gray didn't mind it. The young shifter hadn't had an easy life and if he just wanted to sit and watch the other guests, Gray was okay with that.

He'd be the person who Mark could just be himself with.

"We could try being friends," Mark finally said.

"Okay."

"But that doesn't mean I'll ever want to shift with you."

Gray was disappointed, but he wouldn't let it show. "It'll be your decision. I won't pressure you."

"Thanks," Mark responded. "Maybe someday, though."

Gray hid his smile behind his hand. If he had to guess, he would say that Mark wanted to be able to shift and run with his own kind. Gray would prove to the younger shifter that they would be just fine together. Tyler was right. He was more human than wolf. In the community he was going to live in, he'd probably need to prove that more than once. Gray didn't mind. He would show everyone that he belonged. And Beth belonged with him.

* * * *

The kitchen was quiet and empty, giving Gray his first chance at being alone to gather his thoughts. The sun was setting and, while he'd enjoyed the get-together, he was tired as well.

Plus he hadn't gotten to spend more than a few quick stolen moments with Beth since they'd woken up.

The wake-up had been nice, though. She'd climbed under the covers and he'd woken with her lips wrapped around his morning wood.

"You have a sappy smile on your face," Beth teased, coming up behind him and wrapping her arms around his waist.

"I can't help it. You turned me into a sappy, smiling man," he joked back.

"I thought I just turned you on," she taunted, slipping her hand lower.

"Why, Beth!" he exclaimed with a smile, turning in her arms. "I'm shocked you would try to seduce me with a yard full of people."

She threw her head back and laughed. "Oh, I'm not trying."

She tugged him across the kitchen.

"Where are we...?"

She opened the tall walk-in pantry and shoved him inside.

"The closet, babe?" he chuckled.

"Oh shut up!" she ordered with a smirk, unbuttoning his jeans and finding him already hard. "Or I'll have to shut you up."

As she closed her lips around his cock, he cursed, pleaded and begged. She was not going to shut him up this way. It felt too good to be inside her hot mouth. "People...out...side," he managed to warn.

Beth leaned back, letting his shaft go. "This is a shifters' inn. Every room, including the closets, are soundproofed. Now shut up and enjoy."

"Oh!" He sucked in a breath. "Fuck!"

She didn't even give him time to brace himself. Just took his cock down to the root and swallowed.

"Jesus Christ!"

Beth used the perfect amount of suction while working his balls with one hand. He buried his hands in her hair while thrusting carefully. Gray didn't want to choke her, but he needed just a little more pressure.

He felt the tingle at the base of his spine signaling his release coming and pulled away.

"Why'd you do that?" she asked, still on her knees peering up at him.

"Up!" He helped by dragging her to her feet. "I want inside you."

"I'm not going to argue with that," Beth told him.

"Over here." Spotting a low empty shelf, Gray palmed her lower back until she was bent over. He made quick work of unsnapping her jeans and yanking them down with her panties. Gray slid his fingers through her slick folds, gathering up her juices before plunging one digit inside.

Beth squirmed before arching back.

"You want me?" he teased.

"Always," she responded.

Gray fingered her for several more moments before tugging his hand away and grasping his erection. He positioned himself at the entrance of her pussy then slowly pushed inside.

As he entered her, Beth rose onto her toes.

Once he was buried deep, he gripped Beth's hips tightly before pulling out. He slammed back quickly. The shelf wobbled but held. He repeated his move once, twice. Yes, this was what he needed.

The claiming of Beth, making her his once again, was perfect. He didn't know if he'd ever tire of losing himself with her.

Each time he thrust, she threw herself back, so he slid deep. She was what completed him.

Beth reached behind her, grabbing his thighs. Her nails dug in painfully, but that just had him driving in faster and harder. Arching her back, she cried out while climaxing.

Gray grunted as her body tightened around his cock. He

bit his lip to keep from continuing his lunges. He needed to move, but he wanted to see her sated and know that only he would be giving her pleasure like that.

"Damn," she murmured. He waited until she peered up at him before very slowly withdrawing.

"Not quite finished." He smirked then slammed back inside. He plunged in and out but this time concentrated on his own pleasure instead of hers.

It wasn't long before he growled, threw his head back and came.

With a few erratic strokes, he filled her with his seed. The other shifters would know what they'd been doing and the primal part of him wanted to howl in approval.

He barely kept himself from collapsing on her. This was not the time or place.

"We better get dressed," Beth said. "We may have privacy right now, but I wouldn't rely on it lasting."

Gray chuckled. "This was your idea." He groaned, pulling out and steadying himself.

"Come on, big guy," Beth said, turning, then patted his chest. "I'll get you a beer."

If he couldn't get a nap, he'd have to make do with a beer. "I think you should sit on my lap while I drink it," he said. "Keep me company."

She laughed as he wanted.

"Are you done?" Loud banging on the pantry door. "Everyone's leaving."

"Go away, Kiley!" Gray shouted. "I thought this room was soundproof?"

Beth laughed. She straightened her clothing. "Why would they soundproof a food closet?"

"You little minx!" Gray tugged up his jeans and had them fastened as the door shook.

"No use hiding!" Kiley called. "We already heard!"

"I'm going to kill her," Gray grumbled.

Beth rose to her tiptoes. "Come on!"

Gray expected Kiley to be in the kitchen. Maybe Austin,

since he was never too far from his mate, but he also found Claude, Dorothy, Tyler, Dawson, Casey and Zachary.

"Bunch of perverts," Gray accused.

Dawson grinned at him. "Welcome to the family, wolf."

He couldn't even be mad. Not with Beth in his arms and his old family in the same room as his new. "I hate you all," he lied.

This was what his life was going to be now. A mixture of wolf, feline, bird, fox and many other species all entwined in his life. His *new* life.

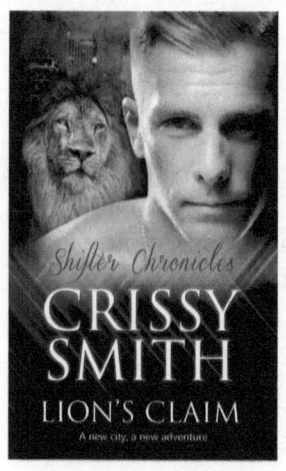

Lion's Claim

Excerpt

Chapter One

The alarm shrieked, scaring Annabelle Sanchez awake and out of bed. She stumbled around the room, dressing quickly. This wasn't the first time and wouldn't be the last that her morning started that way, but it always made her leap up in fear. Her bedside clock read three-fifteen a.m. Having been taught to always be prepared, Annabelle jogged down the hall less than four minutes after the warning call. Doors opened as she passed, signaling others rushing to join her.

Mac Gordon was on his phone as Annabelle ran into the main bar area, Trent, Carter and Kelly spreading out behind her. Trent and Carter each stood next to one of the windows to peer out while Kelly ran to take position by the front door. Annabelle's place was at Mac's side. She would carry out all Mac's orders while directing the rest of the team.

The rumble of motorcycles shook the floorboards where she stood and she recognized the sound of those pipes. At normal times, Annabelle would be comforted by the people who were arriving, but in the middle of the night, with the alarms still ringing, she was filled with dread. There was no reason for two of the team to be coming in hot.

"They're here," Mac said into his cell. "Put everyone else on high alert. We'll take care of things here. Good job."

Mac's words had everyone in the room tensing. Putting the entire town on high alert was a big deal. The town of Brookside had around two hundred residents only, mostly shifters or their loved ones. It was a unique place but perfect for the secrets that had to be kept.

Annabelle wiped her hands down the legs of the sweatpants she'd pulled on. Her heart still pounded. It'd be a long morning and she'd only been in bed for a few short hours.

Mac turned toward them. "We have an emergency case," he said.

"Trouble?" Trent asked. He bounced on his toes as though he itched to get into the thick of things.

"No signs of it so far," Mac told him before glancing at Kelly. "Kelly, can you make some food? They're going to be hungry."

"Of course," Kelly replied, already hurrying toward the kitchen.

"Trent, Carter," Mac said. "Take your bikes and backtrack to the south. Make sure no one followed."

"You got it, boss," Trent responded with a wide grin.

Annabelle knew that he hoped to actually find someone following, and had to shake her head. The hyena shifter was just a little bit crazy at times. Trent gave a quick nod to Carter and the two men stalked toward the back door to follow orders.

"What's going on?" Annabelle asked once she and Mac were alone.

"Not sure," Mac confessed. "Calvin and Duffy have someone with them. Since they didn't call me first, we have to proceed cautiously."

The motorcycles' engines cut off and Annabelle took the time to brace herself for what would be coming through the doors. In the many years she'd worked along with Mac, there hadn't been much she hadn't seen. It was sad to say that nothing surprised Annabelle any longer. People, human or shifter, could be so cruel to one another.

The front door opened and Calvin Montgomery stepped inside first. A young woman with long, flowing red hair had practically attached herself to him. Duffy followed behind the two, pulling the door shut before moving to lean against the wall.

From the front, the bar wasn't much to look at, sure. But as an establishment that welcomed some rough characters nightly, its rundown exterior meant one thing—that whoever set foot inside would be comfortable.

Tabletops might be scarred and the floor scratched, but so what? The important thing about it? That a person's species didn't matter when they walked inside the Den. Everyone was invited to sit and enjoy a good brew.

The woman with Calvin didn't look like she'd ever stepped into a place like their bar before, but that was all right. She wouldn't be on the main floor for long.

Annabelle did her best to appear as non-threatening as possible while taking a few short steps forward. She didn't know the girl's story, but, like all the shifters who came through the Den, this woman needed the kind of help only they could offer.

"Samantha," Calvin said softly. "Annabelle is the one I was telling you about. She'll get you settled."

Annabelle smiled at the redhead. She had beautiful clear green eyes, and freckles across her nose. She couldn't be much older than twenty. "It's nice to meet you, Samantha." She kept her voice gentle.

"Hello," Samantha replied, peeking around Calvin.

"I bet you could use a good meal, a shower and bed." Annabelle waved her hand around. "It might not look like much, but you'll be comfortable here, I promise."

Samantha nodded at her and glanced at Calvin.

"You go ahead with Annabelle," Calvin told her. He motioned to Mac. "That's my boss. I have to tell him what's going on."

"O...okay." Samantha looked at Mac nervously.

Mac might have appeared intimidating with his dark hair and eyes, along with his full beard. A huge, muscular, tattooed biker, to Annabelle he was also the kindest man she'd ever met. Mac smiled encouragement at Samantha. It normally didn't take their guests long to trust him, so Annabelle felt certain that Samantha would soon be one of Mac's biggest fans.

"I can already smell Kelly's cooking," Annabelle said, pulling Samantha's attention to her.

"I am hungry," Samantha admitted, her voice small.

"Well, then," Annabelle said. "Follow me." She led the way out of the main room and past the bar area. Since the bar had closed up hours ago, all the neon signs had been turned off and only a few security lights remained on. Samantha wouldn't ever be in the public part of the bar again. Once through the doors, she'd be kept out of view from anyone who might stumble in or come looking for her.

Behind her, Mac greeted Calvin and Duffy. The back-slapping was boisterous. Calvin and Duffy had been gone two weeks, which wasn't unusual. They loved to travel around on their bikes and, if they weren't needed at home, they might be anywhere in the US. Annabelle envied their freedom, but she had her own reasons for never leaving their small northern California town.

"Hi!" Kelly greeted them warmly as they stepped into the open kitchen.

The space wasn't big and a large stainless-steel oven and fridge dominated the room, but it was inviting. Annabelle always felt warm and comfortable there. While the bar did sell some appetizers and easy items, the real cooking took place once the doors were closed to the public. During the day, Kelly worked as a waitress along with Annabelle, but Kelly loved to cook for the family.

"It smells good," Annabelle praised. "This is Samantha."

"Hi, Samantha." Kelly waved. "Make yourself at home at the table. I'll have something to snack on here in just one minute. I also made a fresh pot of coffee."

"Thank you," Samantha replied quietly. "I hope you didn't go to too much trouble."

"Nah," Kelly said. "I'm glad Calvin and Duffy are back. Plus they brought you, so it gives me an excuse to cook."

Annabelle smiled as she pulled out a chair for Samantha from the table. None of the chairs matched, but that didn't matter. This was where all of the family ate meals together, so there was plenty of room—especially when they never knew who from town might drop by. Kelly really did love cooking for the people she cared about. Before she had joined them, Kelly had cooked in a restaurant, working fourteen or more hours a day. Now she only stood behind the stove when she wanted to.

"Can I get you something to drink?" Annabelle asked Samantha.

When Samantha sat in the chair, with Annabelle still standing behind her, Annabelle picked up the scent of dirt and foliage. *Fox shifter*. Annabelle was surprised. Foxes weren't a very common shifter species and she'd only ever met one other. Annabelle didn't say anything to Samantha about it, though. It wouldn't be comfortable for her to be around such large predatory shifters. Since her own animal was rare and small, Annabelle hoped Samantha would be even more at ease in her presence.

The way Samantha kept her shoulders hunched showed years of wariness from whatever she'd been put through. Even when Annabelle had first been brought to the bar, she'd had a chip on her shoulder. Annabelle didn't cower to anyone.

She might only be five foot six but Annabelle's attitude was big enough to go up against all the huge shifters who surrounded her.

Maybe one day, Samantha would regain her confidence. If anyone could give Samantha the chance of reclaiming her strength, it was them.

"Can I have some water, please?" Samantha asked.

"You got it," Annabelle said, stepping toward the fridge.

The guys would probably start guzzling coffee when they got there, as they'd need the caffeine to keep them up to make plans. Annabelle hoped she'd be able to get some more sleep, so she chose two bottles of water for herself and Samantha.

As she passed by Kelly, she saw a couple of dishes already set on the side. Annabelle picked up one with a variety of cheeses, meats, crackers and fruit and carried it over. Samantha's eyes lit up at the food as Annabelle set it in the middle of the table. Annabelle put down the water bottles then picked up a stack of paper plates from the counter.

"Help yourself," Annabelle told her.

She set the plates down before going back and picking up bowls of chips. Kelly flipped hamburger patties on the grill and Annabelle's stomach started to growl. She'd shifted for several hours earlier but hadn't eaten after since it'd been so late. She was really hungry now that she'd smelled the food.

Samantha loaded a plate with a couple of crackers and a small amount of fruit. Annabelle hoped she'd eat more than that. While the dark circles under Samantha's eyes spoke of her being exhausted, Samantha was also very skinny. Like she hadn't had a good meal in a lot longer than the road trip would have taken.

Annabelle really wanted to know Samantha's story but it wasn't her place to ask. Instead, she took the seat next to Samantha and reached for some of the fruit. She didn't fill the silence with small talk. In her experience, Samantha would be thinking about what she'd run from and what was going to happen now. As much as Annabelle wanted to take Samantha's thoughts away, Annabelle knew she needed to take her cues from Samantha.

"I really appreciate all this," Samantha whispered.

"It's what we do," Annabelle replied honestly.

"I'm glad," Samantha said.

Annabelle patted her shoulder, pleased when Samantha leaned in to her touch instead of flinching away. There were many reasons that the underground organization Mac ran even existed. Mac had been taking in strays, like herself, for years.

She'd been fourteen when Mac had come across her living in an alley, sleeping behind a Dumpster. After running away from her twelfth foster home, Annabelle was not going to go back into the system. Mac had offered her an alternative. And it wasn't sick and twisted the way all the other offers she'd gotten had been. Mac had just opened the Den and needed help with the nephew he had custody of. Duffy had been seven when Mac had brought Annabelle home. Now, thirteen years later, this group was the family she loved, the only one she'd ever had.

Mac, Calvin and Duffy walked into the room and Annabelle smiled up at them. Mac was the father figure who'd raised her, made sure she had enough to eat, a place to sleep, love and affection. Duffy was a little brother to her. When Duffy had fallen in love with Calvin, Annabelle had had another brother. The others in the group were like cousins, uncles, aunts and other extended family members. It was all she'd ever wanted. Getting to help shifters in trouble gave her an extra purpose. She felt as if she was making the world a better place.

Calvin ran his fingers across Annabelle's shoulder before he took a seat on the other side of Samantha, with Duffy and Mac sitting across from them. Even if trouble had come home with Calvin and Duffy, she was happy they'd returned.

"Feeling better?" Calvin asked Samantha quietly.

"Yes, thank you," Samantha replied. She looked at Mac. "Thank you for taking me in."

"Of course," Mac said. "We want to help in any way that we can."

Samantha nodded.

"Burgers!" Kelly announced, carrying a platter of meat and buns to the table.

"Oh, God," Calvin moaned. "I missed your cooking."

"Me, too," Duffy agreed, already reaching for the food.

Mac slapped his hand. "Ladies first," he growled. "Didn't I teach you manners?"

Duffy gave Mac a sheepish grin. "Sorry, but if I'd had to eat fast food one more day, I was going to do something drastic, like order a salad."

Everyone laughed, including Samantha, which seemed to be the break in tension that they'd needed. They began to eat. The food disappeared quickly while Annabelle shared looks and smiles with the group. The loneliness that usually surrounded her was absent. At least for a while. Eventually Calvin and Duffy would return to the road, Kelly would be buried in a cookbook, trying to find new recipes, and Mac's job would have him stressed and locked in his office. But, for the moment, her family was with her and that made her content.

By the time their stomachs were full, Samantha's head bobbed in exhaustion.

"Hey." Annabelle laid her palm against Samantha's back. "How about I show you to your room and let you shower and get some sleep?"

"That'd be great," Samantha said.

Annabelle stood, glancing at Mac. He gave her a discreet nod to take Samantha downstairs. They guys would make sure that there was no lingering trace of Samantha, including her scent. Samantha gazed around as they walked through the narrow hallway that led to the bedrooms. Six of their group lived on that level. As far as anyone knew, they were the only ones who resided in the back rooms.

A mist sprayed over their heads and Samantha flinched.

"A scent neutralizer," Annabelle explained. "No one will ever know you were here."

Samantha laughed nervously. "Okay."

"This way," Annabelle said when they reached the end of the corridor. She moved aside a picture of the family to reveal a security panel. Before she punched in the four numbers needed, she glanced over her shoulder at Samantha. "Ready?"

Samantha's eyes were wide, but she nodded in response.

Excitement coursed through Annabelle. She loved going down to the lower level. It looked like an entirely different building. While the bar appeared rundown and barely able to keep standing, that was just the surface appearance. The modern high-tech of the converted basement was amazing.

She tapped in the code and the wood separated, revealing a three-inch-thick steel door. Annabelle stepped forward to run her hands over the shiny barrier until she found the notch where the latch was located. She pulled down and a click sounded before the door unlocked.

"Wow!" Samantha murmured.

"Just wait," Annabelle said.

She had to push the door open, but it moved inward silently and smoothly. As soon as she placed her foot inside, the motion sensor light triggered, illuminating the entry to the underground bunker.

Down here was a whole different world. The walls were solid concrete to keep those who needed to hide safe and out of view. But the homey feel of the space surprised most people.

The barrier opened into a large living area. Black leather couches and chairs were scattered around the room, alongside heavy, dark-wood furniture. Directly across the room was a small kitchen area and off to one side, the office had been set up. Monitors lined the walls, showing feeds from the numerous security cameras around the property. The hum of the computers was the only sound in the quiet space.

"Let me show you where you can sleep," Annabelle said. Samantha remained standing in the doorway. When she moved forward, Annabelle pushed the door closed until she heard the locks reengage. On the other side, the wood panel would be back in place. "There are three bedrooms down here. Someone will be out here in the main room at all times."

"You do this a lot," Samantha commented.

"Yes," Annabelle admitted. There was no reason to lie.

"When Cal and Duffy offered to get me to safety, I had no idea all this existed." She waved her hand around. "I don't... I don't know what to do."

Annabelle took her hand and drew her to the couch. It sounded as though Samantha needed to talk to someone. They sank into the big comfortable cushions, which was one of the best feelings in the world to Annabelle. "All you have to do relax, trust that we know what we're doing and get some rest. Before you know it, you'll have a brand-new life."

"How can you do all this?" Samantha asked.

It was a common question. "Each one of us has our own reasons for getting involved in this organization. In the beginning, when Mac first set this up as a safe house, we mainly dealt with domestic disputes. Women who needed to get away from an abusive husband or boyfriend. Because of our animal sides, it can be harder for a shifter to escape. Most of us have it bred into us to listen to our Alpha, the dominant, or whatever we have. It's difficult to fight back when that person is the abuser."

"Yeah, it is," Samantha whispered.

Annabelle remained holding Samantha's hand and the fox shifter began to squeeze harder.

"After the humans were told about the existence of shifters, we expanded. Sometimes the laws don't protect us. It's a sad but true fact. We help those who need a new life." Annabelle believed in what they did. She'd seen too many men, women and children come through those doors who'd had no hope until Mac had worked his magic and found them a place where they might regain the life that had been stolen from them.

"You didn't ask me what happened," Samantha whispered.

"Because you don't have to tell me," Annabelle assured her. "If you don't ever want to think about it again, you don't have to. But if you want to talk to someone, I am more than happy to listen. I've been told I'm pretty good at it." She offered what she hoped came off as an encouraging smile.

"I'm pregnant," Samantha said, placing her hand protectively across her stomach.

"Oh!" Annabelle reached over and laid her palm to cover Samantha's. "A baby!"

"If I'd stayed, I would lose this child like I did my first one. He would have beaten me until I miscarried again."

"Your husband?" Annabelle asked gently.

"No," Samantha said. "I wouldn't marry him, but he refused let me go. My brother Mike got money and a high position in our troop. He's the only family I had. He turned his back on me, though. I begged for help, but all my brother cared about was moving up in rank."

"I'm so sorry." Annabelle felt tears gathering.

"I thought, when I got pregnant the first time, the abuse would stop. I honestly believed Frank would be happy about a child. I couldn't have been more wrong. He was furious. Frank wouldn't allow anyone or anything to take my attention from him."

Annabelle had heard similar stories before, but this still sickened and shocked her. "No one helped?" She didn't know why she'd asked. A part of her just wanted to hear that someone had attempted to come to this poor girl's defense.

"No one's going to report a crime the sheriff was responsible for," Samantha said.

Fuck. Annabelle scooted over and tugged Samantha close until the little fox shifter sobbed against her shoulder. Once again, someone was using the law to protect themselves instead of the innocent. In Annabelle's experience, she'd never come across an honest police official. That was why the group did what they did.

She waited until Samantha's crying jag finished before pulling away. "If you could go anywhere in the world, where would it be?" she asked.

Samantha shook her head. "No idea. I just want to live somewhere private where no one will bother me. I want to raise my child in a loving home."

Annabelle grinned. "You'll get that."

"How can you be so sure?"

"Because our network is vast," Annabelle said. "You'll end up right where you're supposed to. I believe that with all my heart."

"I have a hard time trusting any of this. The entire ride here I expected Frank or my brother to come after us," Samantha confessed. "I still expect them to come busting in."

"They won't," Annabelle assured her.

"How can you know that?"

"Others have tried," Annabelle told her. "No one has ever gotten down here. You're safe." Even if the bar was breached, no one would find the entrance to the lower level. They'd run tests and drills, making sure.

Samantha nodded. "If your two friends hadn't come across Frank beating me in a parking lot, I don't know what might have happened."

"How'd they get you out of there?"

"Calvin jumped in and saved me. He kept punching Frank until Frank fell to the ground. The restaurant was closed and none of the troop was there because we weren't even supposed to be out of our territory. I'd run off because I found out I'm pregnant and Frank didn't want the others to know that I'd taken off on him again. Duffy stepped in front of me, sort of guarding me, in case Frank got up."

"Sound like our guys," Annabelle commented.

"I wish he'd killed Frank," Samantha whispered the admission.

"I understand." Annabelle meant it, too.

"Instead, once Frank was unconscious, Calvin turned to me and said, 'If you want to leave here, we have somewhere safe we can take you. If not, we'll leave you alone. It's your choice, but you have to make it now.' So I chose to go with them."

"I'm glad you did."

"Me, too," Samantha replied. "I think I'd like to shower now."

"Good," Annabelle said. She rose, pulling Samantha up with her.

The first room was the largest and also had the biggest bathroom, so Annabelle led Samantha in that direction. *Samantha deserves some pampering.*

"Here," Annabelle said, pushing open the bedroom door. The décor was soft blues that she had read somewhere would give the space a relaxing atmosphere. Mac had allowed Annabelle to fix up the rooms. She hoped the people who stayed there found them peaceful.

"It's beautiful," Samantha praised.

"There are clean clothes in the dresser. We have all different sizes, so take whatever you want," Annabelle said. "The bathroom is stocked with everything you should need."

Samantha turned to her. "Thank you."

"You're very welcome," Annabelle pulled her into a quick hug before stepping out and closing the door behind her.

Trent and Carter would return at any minute, so they'd probably head down there. Carter took care of the group's IT needs. He'd no doubt be watching the cameras for the next several hours. Annabelle walked toward the little kitchen area with its fridge, microwave, stove and small pantry. Kelly was really good at keeping it stocked so that if they had emergency cases like Samantha, the group was prepared.

Annabelle started a pot of coffee before walking to the couch. She picked up the blanket off the back and wrapped it around herself, then lay her head against the arm. She was really tired.

She heard the water turn on in Samantha's room. The rooms down there weren't soundproofed, because part of watching over their charges meant whoever was on guard duty needed to hear what happened inside the other rooms. Sometimes the people who came to them for help became so overwhelmed that they tried to harm themselves.

Not hearing anything to worry about, Annabelle closed her eyes.

The adrenaline from earlier was slowly leaving, making her body feel heavy. It had been a couple of months since they'd had anyone needing their help. Sometimes it happened like that. They'd go for a while without any guests, or sometimes they'd be spread thin by having more than one person who needed assistance.

During the times when it was just her small family around, they played in their shifted forms and worked the bar. The residents in Brookside were all shifters. No humans stayed longer than a few nights. It was the town secret, so that when humans showed up, the population of the small quiet town didn't do anything to draw attention to their differences. It was a shifter's choice whether he or she decided to be out in public or not. The inhabitants of Brookside all kept their shifter ability secret. It allowed them to remain safe.

The locks disengaging caught her attention and she opened her eyes. Carter walked in first with Trent right behind him, which didn't surprise her. She hadn't been expecting Mac, Calvin or Duffy, though. Mac cocked his head, no doubt listening to where Samantha had gotten off to, and nodded.

"She's showering? Good. That should help her relax. How's she doing?" Mac asked, striding toward where

Annabelle sat.

"Yes," Annabelle said. They'd have a few minutes to talk without Samantha hearing them. "I think she's doing okay. A little scared about what's going to happen but grateful that she got away."

"It was lucky we came across her," Calvin commented. He sat in the chair next to the couch.

"You're her hero," Annabelle teased.

Calvin just shook his head.

"You should have seen him," Duffy said, dropping down beside her on the couch. He pulled her legs onto her lap to rub the soles of her feet. "He was a total badass."

"Which you need to be careful about," Mac told Calvin. "You could have gotten yourself arrested or worse."

"I know, boss. I saw him hit her and lost it. Samantha was so much smaller than this guy. He was at least six foot two and two hundred and eight pounds."

"Damn," Annabelle said. "She can't be more than five two and I'd be surprised if she weighed more than one ten."

"Yeah," Calvin said. He looked at Mac. "I know I messed up. We tried to cover our tracks, but I don't know if we got away clean. He's a fucking sheriff. I'm sorry."

"It's okay." Mac grasped Calvin's shoulder, giving him a firm squeeze. Annabelle watched as Mac turned fatherly. "We can handle it. The important thing is you brought that girl here and you and Duffy are safe."

"I'll make up for it," Calvin promised.

"Cal," Mac said, moving to crouch in front of him. "There's nothing to make up for. Yes, you made some mistakes, but I'm proud of you. If someone had stepped in when the same thing was happening with my sister, she'd still be here."

Duffy's hand tightened on her foot. It wasn't often that Mac brought up Charlotte's murder. A sweet girl killed by her jealous husband who'd been abusing her for years. Mac had still been in the army and hadn't seen Charlotte much, and he'd had no idea what she'd been dealing with. Not until he'd gotten the call that she was dead, killed by her husband, before he'd turned the gun on himself. Duffy had been found hiding in his closet, a scared and traumatized boy.

"Mac," Calvin whispered.

"I hope this fucker does come here," Mac said, menacingly pounding a fist into the palm of his other hand. "We'll show him what's it's like to fight someone his own size."

Calvin nodded. "Okay."

"Why don't you two go get cleaned up and some sleep? Trent and Carter are on the cameras," Mac said.

"Yeah." Calvin ran his hands roughly over his face.

Duffy patted her leg before rising.

Annabelle waited until Calvin and Duffy had left, the door closing behind them, to peer up at Mac. "You okay?" She glanced into the office area, but Trent and Carter were busy on the computers.

Mac sighed deeply and dropped down into the chair that Calvin had sat in earlier. "I have a really bad feeling about this."

"What? Why?" She straightened up.

"I don't know," Mac said. "I just feel like this isn't going to be a simple case."

"We'll be okay, though, right? We'll get Samantha out of here?"

"Oh you can count on that." Mac leaned forward, dropping his hands between his knees. "I'll never let anyone hurt any of you. We have to move fast and cover our tracks, but Samantha is going to be safe. She and the baby will have a good life."

Annabelle bit her lip. Now she was scared. If Mac had any concern about Samantha's situation, then Annabelle needed to consider what might happen. If any strangers showed up she'd keep her eye on them. No one was going to threaten what they were doing there.

More books from Crissy Smith

Book one in the Were Chronicles series

Marissa Boyd finds herself drawn into a world she can never be a part of, complete with an Alpha wolf who takes whatever he wants. And he wants her.

Book two in the Were Chronicles series

Enforcing his control never felt better

Book three in the Were Chronicles series

*Adam White is the new Alpha in his territory but Tasha
Johnson is the one in charge.*

Book four in the Were Chronicles series

The Rogue meets the Alpha…and their worlds explode.

About the Author

Crissy Smith

Crissy Smith lives in Texas with her husband, daughter, and three Labrador retrievers. The three dogs love to curl up under her computer desk and nap while she writes. It doesn't leave a lot of room for her but what's a woman to do?

When not writing or reading, she enjoys hunting, camping and shooting. But she has a girly side too and is addicted to pedicures and coffee.

She has been writing since she was a teenager and still loves everything to do with the paranormal. Her stories and characters all have a place in her heart. She loves the alpha male, the dominant werewolf, or the Master vampire which find their way in most of her books.

Learn more about the characters she has created at her website where they have their very own page. It will be updated from time to time to let you know what's going on with them. You can also find out who will be in the next book.

Crissy Smith loves to hear from readers. You can find contact information, website details and an author profile page at https://www.totallybound.com/